A Child. Yelena's Child.

How had he missed *that?*

A deathly calm swept in to cleave his entire body, slicing at his control and reopening past wounds all over again.

"How old?" he finally asked.

She actually had the audacity to lift that proud chin of hers, to meet his glare with one of her own. "Five months."

As his mind did the math then double-checked, a thin film of rage clouded his vision, choking him into silence. If he'd had any smidgen of doubt about his plans, any tiny attack of conscience, she'd well and truly obliterated them.

The night Yelena had declared she loved him, she'd been pregnant with another man's child.

Dear Reader,

What a crazy year it's been! Writing Alex and Yelena's story has been anything but a smooth road—among other things I've been quarantined, slammed with flu, chicken-poxed (not mine!) and crashed via computer...not to mention those crazy school holidays when nothing seems to get done. Such speed bumps are a good reminder of where your priorities lie. And in their own way, my hero and heroine hold family above all else—a value I'm sure many of you can agree with!

I'm especially pleased to bring you a story that features two major Australian contrasts—our capital city, Canberra, and iconic Ayers Rock (or Uluru, as we Aussies call it). Rest assured I spent many hours researching to make Diamond Falls a uniquely breathtaking place that sets the scene for Alex and Yelena's romance. I hope you're drawn in to their world as much as I was.

As a bonus, you can drop by www.outbackbillionairesandbabies.wordpress.com where Robyn Grady, Maxine Sullivan and I have set up home for our three special BILLIONAIRES AND BABIES books.

With love,

Paula x

www.paularoe.com

PAULA ROE

THE BILLIONAIRE BABY BOMBSHELL

Published by Silhouette Books
America's Publisher of Contemporary Romance

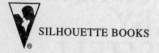

SILHOUETTE BOOKS

ISBN-13: 978-0-373-73033-9

Recycling programs
for this product may
not exist in your area.

THE BILLIONAIRE BABY BOMBSHELL

Visit Silhouette Books at www.eHarlequin.com

Printed in U.S.A.

Books by Paula Roe

Silhouette Desire

Forgotten Marriage #1824
Boardrooms & a Billionaire Heir #1867
The Magnate's Baby Promise #1962
The Billionaire Baby Bombshell #2020

PAULA ROE

Despite wanting to be a vet, choreographer, card shark, hairdresser and an interior designer (although not simultaneously!) British-born, Aussie-bred Paula ended up as a personal assistant, office manager, software trainer and aerobics instructor for thirteen interesting years.

Paula lives in western New South Wales, Australia, with her family, two opinionated cats and a garden full of dependent native birds. She still retains a deep love of filing systems, stationery and traveling, even though the latter doesn't happen nearly as often as she'd like. She loves to hear from her readers—you can visit her at her Web site at www.paularoe.com.

My deepest thanks to all who've helped me with this book, in particular Lis Hoorweg for her knowledge of Canberra and its surrounds, Monique Wood for her insights into the mysterious world of public relations and Linley for her always awesome brainstorming skills. And Dad, for explaining the complexities of shares, partnerships and business practices (and no, this doesn't mean you have to read the book!).

Special mention goes to Maxine Sullivan and Robyn Grady— your support and encouragement always lift my heart.

And lastly, to my fabulous editor, Charles—here's to our first book together and the many more to follow!

One

"You didn't say yes?" Yelena Valero whirled from the unrestrained twentieth-floor view of Canberra's Lake Burley Griffin to her boss's inscrutable countenance. "Tell me you didn't say Bennett & Harper PR would take on Alexander Rush as a client."

"No." Behind his desk Jonathon Harper's bushy eyebrows took a dive as he reclined in the leather chair. "*You* said yes. Rush made it perfectly clear it's you or no account."

The air sped from her lungs, momentarily disorienting her. In the next instant her heart kicked in, an insistent thump-thump against her ribs. "Jon...you know we had history—he was involved with my sister—"

"And I really don't care. You've known him since, what—tenth grade?"

"Yes, but I really don't think—"

"Here are his clippings." Jon tossed a file on his desk. "This is non-negotiable, Yelena," he added pointedly before she could say another word. "I gave you six months off, no questions. You want to be considered for partner now? You clear your schedule. What Alex Rush wants, you give him."

With a final wave of his hand, he turned back to his computer, dismissing her.

Yelena glared at his perfectly groomed head for a few seconds before sweeping up the file and turning on her heel.

By the time she'd stalked down the hall, her high heels clicking out her fury on the cool slate floor, reality had swept in to douse every irrational thought.

She ground to a stop, staring at her closed office door at the end of the silent hallway. If she was Jonathon's partner, his equal, he'd never have played her. But the man obviously thought her and Alex's tenacious past was an advantage, not the major train wreck Yelena knew it was.

She closed her eyes and took a deep breath.

One, two, three. Her stomach tossed with shock, fear—and...

Four, five, six.

—a queasy sense of exhilaration. *Wait, what?*

She frowned, scrunching up her face.

Eight, nine.

Ten.

After a slow exhale she breathed in again. The relaxation technique finally began to kick in, calming her pulse, regulating her breathing.

Slowly she opened her eyes and focused on her door. Alex Rush represented the unknown. He'd always been a threat to her control, yet time and again she'd ignored the warnings.

But she desperately needed this promotion. The freedom it would give far outweighed any monetary compensation— freedom to set her own hours, to work from home. To pick and choose her own clients. To prove to her very traditional parents that she didn't need a rich husband to keep her in dresses and spa treatments. And above all, it meant she could be a proper mother instead of an absent one.

As she pulled her back straight and gently rolled her neck for good measure, she felt the familiar pop of muscles through her shoulders. Then she stalked the rest of the way to her office with more decisiveness than she felt.

Alex Rush stood alone in Yelena's simple, almost austere office, his back deliberately to the door. He knew the huge window, one that took in Canberra's Parliament House in its commanding August morning glory, haloed his height to strategic effect. He needed all the power and authority his size projected, needed to put her at a mental disadvantage, to show he was in control and calling the shots.

His confidence had briefly bowed to uncharacteristic hesitation before he'd determinedly swept the doubts aside. *No time for second thoughts.* Yelena and her brother Carlos had dug their hole so they only had themselves to blame.

The swift click of heels against tiles broke through his subconscious and in the next instant the door whooshed open with an efficient shove.

Game on.

To his irritation, his heart rate rocketed, bathing his body in anticipatory warmth.

"Jonathon tells me you asked for me personally, Alex. Mind telling me why?"

He slowly turned, bracing for battle. Yet for all his mental preparation, he was woefully unprepared for the breathless impact that seeing Yelena Valero always evoked. The solid, pounding heat, the thud his blood made as it sped through his veins—hot, arousing—as if he were a teenager again and seeing her for the first time.

Yelena was drop-dead gorgeous. Sure, the fashionistas would declare her too curvy, her hair too wild, her jaw too square, her lips too full compared with her younger sister's sleekly polished looks. Yet the sight of her always managed to stop his breath.

You're not seventeen anymore. Yelena dumped and betrayed you, siding with Carlos—the man who's hell-bent on destroying you. She's nothing more than a way to make her lying bastard of a brother pay.

A thread of intense fury whipped out, blinding him to everything else. He let it sit there for a heartbeat, tasting the bitterness, almost relishing it, before efficiently stuffing it back into that special place in his mind. Compartmentalizing, his attorney had declared, as if the revelation had deserved a standing ovation.

No one knew he'd spent years perfecting an airtight mask of composure. And by God, he wouldn't lose it now, even though the reckless temptation to reach out and kiss Yelena senseless snaked through his body, forcing his muscles into a tight clench.

"Who let you in my office?" she asked suddenly.

"Jonathan."

She fell silent, the stillness lengthening as she blinked slowly, a small furrow creasing her brows.

"It's been a while, Yelena."

Her eyes narrowed at his inane comment, as if they were seeking the hidden meaning behind his smooth words.

"I hadn't noticed." She stared at her desk then pointedly at him as he remained still, blocking her way.

Not noticed? Fury burnt away the residual lust that had pooled in his brain. He'd done nothing *but* notice the passage of time since his nightmare had begun. His entire world had crashed on Christmas Eve and Yelena…well, she'd simply moved on as if he'd been a temporary pit stop on her journey to the top.

Sharp pain shot through his hands and he glanced down. He'd tightened them into fists.

With an inward curse he forced himself to relax, sweeping

his gaze down her body, knowing she'd take umbrage with his perusal. From her black high heels, the snug grey skirt and matching jacket loosely tied at the waist to the fire-engine red shirt that looked so soft his fingers briefly retightened, she was business personified. Her wild hair was smoothly tied back, makeup subdued. Even her jewelry—small gold hoop earrings and a simple chain with the familiar blue eye of Horus—signaled restraint. So unlike the Yelena he knew, the woman with the wild kisses and hot skin, the sultry take-hold-of-your-groin-and-squeeze laugh.

The one who'd dropped him like a ten-ton millstone when he'd been accused of murdering his father.

She scowled and crossed her arms, dragging him back to the present. "Have you quite finished?"

He allowed himself a smile. "Oh, not by a long shot."

Before she could say anything he stepped aside, leaving her to her personal space. With slow deliberation, he lowered himself into one of her guest chairs.

She settled behind that titanic desk, her eyes on him, a wary cat assessing a potential threat. The privileged, spoilt daughter of Ambassador Juan Ramerez Valero, wary? The thought astonished even as it empowered.

"Nice office." He flicked his gaze over the room. "Nice desk. Must've cost a bit."

"Of all the experienced reps in Bennett & Harper, why did you ask for me? Wouldn't our history bother you?"

"Still as blunt as always, I see," Alex murmured, unsurprised.

She crossed her arms and awaited his answer in loaded silence.

"You're one of the best," he stated, deliberately playing to her vanity. "I've been watching your campaign for that singer—Kyle Davis, right? Getting the public to do a one-eighty on a tax cheat was impressive. What you can do for me completely outweighs any—" he paused, his gaze feathering across her mouth before going back to her eyes "—past history."

He knew his subtle ego stroking fell way short when she met his eyes head on, unblinking. He'd never been subjected to her "Queen of Silence" look but he'd seen it focused on others. It was a look meant to fluster and embarrass, usually given after an improper or rude comment. It was all in the steady stare, the slight curve of her eyebrow. And the expectant stillness as cool as the steel from the ancient swords that adorned her father's study.

Yet he easily held her gaze until she was the one forced to break the silence.

"And what exactly would you be hiring me to do?"

"What you're renowned for—positive spin. And, of course, discretion."

"Spin for you?"

"And my mother and sister."

"I see."

Yelena remained calm as, with one fluid movement, he crossed his ankles, then his arms. A perfect image of untouchable male confidence and control, one that ran roughshod over their furtive weeks of intense pre-Christmas passion as if it'd just been something she'd dreamt up.

The guilt-ridden ghosts of her past reared up under his silent inspection, astounding her. Alex Rush had been completely off-limits. Yet that hadn't stopped her from falling for her sister's boyfriend.

She swallowed heavily. *Get a grip.* He was here for business, nothing more. Whatever they'd shared was temporary. Dead and buried.

"You owe me, Yelena."

She stared at him, the startling cut stabbing deep. Damn him for going there and putting a voice to her guilt. As she warred with her conscience, he added, "And you know my family, which will make your job easier."

"Not very well."

"More than most," he countered. "And *we're* familiar with each other."

He made the word *familiar* sound much dirtier than it should. Those arresting, come-to-bed azure eyes, combined with the subtle dip in his voice, did something terrible to her body. Terrible in a wonderful way.

"So your silence means you're taking my account?" he finally said.

She wrenched her gaze from his and picked up her pen to give her nervous hands something to do.

"B&H would be crazy to turn down the son of William Rush, the founder of Australia's leading airline company," she returned calmly. No reason to elaborate, to confirm that her boss had used her partnership application as leverage.

Instinctively her hand sought out her necklace, to rub the Horus pendant dangling there. And just like a magnet, that small movement commanded Alex's eyes.

She abruptly stilled. Fiddling with that pendant was a nervous tic, Alex had laughingly pointed out years ago. *Words can lie but your body can't.* The tic said she was unsure, out of her depth. Conflicted.

His knowing eyes shot to her face and suddenly the memories streamed in, flushing her skin and warming her body in places she'd closed off these last eight months.

"Did you discuss any details with Jonathon?" She said firmly pulling her diary across the desk.

"No."

"Okay." She flicked open the diary and scribbled a few notes, then looked up. "I'll need a few days to get a team together then I can schedule you in for next week—"

"No." He leaned forward and Yelena only just managed to resist scooting back. Even with her huge desk between them, she still felt...vulnerable somehow. As if there was nothing to stop him from leaning across the oak expanse and kissing her.

Her pulse leapt to life, her breath stuttering for one brief second. Ridiculous. Alex Rush was here as a client. She would put his feather in her professional cap, get her promotion and move on. It wasn't personal. Not anymore.

"You can't make next week?" she asked, squelching her body's disturbing reactions.

"We need to start now. Jonathon assured me I would be your only priority."

Yelena tightened her jaw. *Damn you, Jonathon.* "Fine. So let's start."

"Good." He rested his elbows on his knees, snaring her in his gaze. "As you know, the Rush name has had some adverse press these last few months."

Understatement of the year. "I understand you were questioned, suspected but never formally charged for your father's death. It was finally ruled as accidental."

His bright eyes narrowed. "Many people, including a few media outlets, still believe I got away with murder."

I don't. The automatic reply lay on the tip of her tongue but she quickly swallowed it. They both knew the answer. "I'm sorry, Alex."

"What?" His eyebrows went up, cynicism creasing his brow. "You're not going to ask?"

She blinked. "I don't need to."

"Oh, that's right. You were my alibi. Or at least, you would've been if you hadn't suddenly left the country that night."

"Alex…" She leaned back in her chair as his harsh accusation tore into the half-healed wound. "I tried to…I—"

"By the way, how was your holiday? Europe, wasn't it?" His words, although polite, were tinged with barely hidden disdain, sending her heart clunking against her ribcage.

"My…?" *He didn't know.* Well, how could he? Her father

had never issued a press release, though not through Yelena's lack of pleading. To anyone interested enough to inquire, Gabriela was backpacking in blissful anonymity through Asia, absent from the headlines.

Just as they'd always wanted.

"What?" He raised one derisive eyebrow. "You had some sudden life-or-death situation overseas so you just left without even the courtesy of a phone call?"

She clamped down on a dozen furious comebacks, testing the words on her tongue. "I was with Gabriela."

"I see. And how is my footloose ex-girlfriend? I'm assuming she found someone else to be her handbag because I've heard nothing." His mouth thinned, as if barely able to contain his scorn.

You have to stop this. Now. She slapped her hands on the desk, stared at the polished wooden surface and took a deep breath.

"Don't go there, Alex." She managed to rip her eyes away from his piercing blue ones and snap her diary shut with firm finality. "You hired me to do a job. If I'm to do it, we need to leave our personal lives out of it—including whatever issues you and Carlos have."

His gaze turned sharp. "What issues would they be?"

"I have no idea. The last time I saw him was two months ago."

Did he know how much that wounded her, having Carlos lock her out of his life? Apart from a few throwaway comments, she had no idea what her brother's relationship with Alex was since Alex's return to Canberra. Which was a good thing, she decided. She'd grown up this past year—becoming a mother and moving out of the Valero home had not only provided the independence she craved: it had also put a stop to Carlos's stifling "big brother" routine. And she'd banned Alex from her mind, preferring not to know what he was doing or whom he was seeing.

As he considered her with intense scrutiny, the atmosphere slowly disintegrated. It was like…expectancy. As if he wanted to ask a million questions but something held him back. Definitely not the Alex she knew.

"I'll need to speak with your family," she said abruptly.

And just like that, their moment was gone.

"Of course." His expression smoothed and he stood, startling her. "I've arranged an 11:00 a.m. flight." He glanced at his watch. "I'll have a car pick you up from your apartment at ten."

She blinked. "I'm sorry? I thought—"

"You. Me. Flight at eleven," he repeated succinctly. "You need to meet my family—your clients. They're at Diamond Bay."

"Your outback resort?" she asked faintly.

"The same. Don't be late."

"What…" She shook her head, frowning. "What about my team?"

"I need to get back to the resort. Plus my staff is fielding a million calls, so right now, I need one hundred percent discretion. At this moment, *you* are the team."

Of all the—! She shot to her feet. "I can't do everything myself! I need an assistant, an event planner…"

He waved away her protest with a regal hand. "I have ample staff for that. And once we have a firm schedule, you can delegate."

She stared at him. "I have a *life,* a—"

"I thought your work was your life." His chilly appraisal brushed over her almost insultingly.

She crossed her arms. "You don't know anything about me anymore."

"That's true."

The sudden drop in temperature did nothing to cool the slow burn creeping up her neck. Yet before she could form a retort, he reached into his jacket and removed his mobile phone. "Pack for a week. I'll see you at the airport."

Then he was gone, the only evidence of his presence the very male notes of a lingering aftershave.

Yelena was left staring at her open door, stuck in a deep frown that sent tiny aching shards into her temples.

Stop scowling, Yelena. You'll give yourself wrinkles.

Her mother's familiar command cut into her thoughts like diamonds on glass and she automatically smoothed out her features.

How on earth could she leave the past behind and concentrate on her job when this was the result of their proximity?

She'd packed a lifetime of living into the last year. She'd lost a sister and Alex. Even Carlos had drifted away; he'd become so publicity conscious, and the only time they talked these days was to argue. She'd disappointed her family, her life had shattered then been fused back together in irregular mismatched pieces. Like an expensive vase outwardly displaying a flawless façade, only to reveal the hairline cracks on the inside.

Yet Yelena had finally gained control. And she'd become a mother. Through it all, Bella had been worth everything she'd suffered.

She had to do this for Bella.

As she tidied her desk, grabbed her iPhone and locked up, she remained focused on that one honest truth.

Alex Rush was the Holy Grail of clients. His campaign would cement her career and her promotion. And despite his unspoken yet obvious falling out with Carlos, despite their torrid history, he'd chosen her. If he could make this just about business, then so could she. She wasn't about to blow her future on the mistakes of her past.

Two

"I'm just about to feed Bella," Melanie, her neighbor and babysitter, announced from the kitchen as Yelena walked in her front door. "You want?"

Yelena dropped her bag on the counter then took the warm formula from her neighbor with a smile. "Of course. Did my mum call in?"

"She phoned just after you left this morning…" Mel trailed off as she followed Yelena down the quiet hallway and into Bella's room.

"And? Hello, gorgeous girl—how's my *bella* Bella today?" Yelena reached into the crib, scooping up the gurgling five-month-old baby with a theatrical gasp. "You are so big! How did you get to be so big? What did she say, Mel?"

The woman pulled a thread from her tank top's hem, giving the task entirely too much attention. "She said she was coming down with a cold and didn't want to give it to Bella."

"I see." Despite knowing exactly what her mother was like, Yelena's heart still squeezed painfully. Maria Valero played tennis and had a personal fitness trainer. She'd been a three-step-skin-care woman since her teens, she took vitamins, ate just enough to stay healthy, eschewed caffeine, chocolate and other skin-destroying addictions. The woman was going to outlive everyone including, she suspected, Bella.

The lie still had the power to hurt, which meant it still mattered.

"Better to be on the safe side," Melanie added diplomatically as she handed Yelena a cotton towel. "Babies can pick up things so easily."

"That's true." Yelena settled in the huge rocker, gently placing the squirming baby on the nursing pillow that Mel arranged under her arm. When Bella's tiny rosebud mouth latched onto the bottle, something deep and primeval sucker-punched her low.

Fierce and total adoration engulfed her as she gazed down at the feeding baby. She'd do anything for Bella. Her world began and ended with this little girl.

"So what's this business trip you're taking?"

Yelena's gaze remained riveted on Bella, smiling at the baby's gentle slurp. "Just a new client."

"For how long?"

"I should be back next Monday."

"So…" Melanie frowned. "Who's going to look after Bella for a week? Your mum?"

Yelena shook her head. "Can you honestly see her coping with a baby?" *And I wouldn't dream of leaving Bella with a woman who rarely had time for her own children.* "No, Bella's coming with me."

"Wow." Melanie crossed her arms and perched her bottom on the arm of the one-seater. "I didn't know B&H had a nanny service. I'm so in the wrong profession."

"They don't—the resort we're staying at has. And as it's extended travel, B&H foot the bill. Anyway," Yelena said, grinning and gently wiping drool from the baby's mouth, "don't tell me you'd rather work in my frivolous, soulless profession than go back to your thankless, underpaid teaching career."

Melanie's grin matched her friend's at their shared joke. "Nah. And it's not like Matt can't afford to keep me, being head of oncology and all. Plus I get to be a hands-on mum and pick Ben up from kindy. Best of both worlds."

"Well, after this client, I'm expecting that promotion to kick in."

"And about time, too. You work twice as hard as anyone in that firm. But I will miss Bella—she's adorable." She gently stroked the infant's downy head before winking at Yelena. "Even if she does look like her mother."

Deep protectiveness surged, and Yelena answered with a smile. "Hey, can you do me a favor and pack a few things for her while I finish up here?"

While Melanie gathered up clothes and feeding equipment, Yelena burped Bella. Sitting here in the comfort of her daughter's girly lemon-and-white bedroom, it was so very easy to ignore the world. Bella *was* her whole world, from the moment she'd been born. She'd made a promise to that squirming little bundle, wrapped warmly in a birthing blanket.

I'll protect you, keep you safe from harm. And I will always, always be there whenever you need me.

She'd been doing fine until Alex Rush had waltzed back into her life and demanded her complete attention.

Bella sneezed and Yelena gently turned her, bringing the chubby face in line with hers. The baby's thickly lashed brown eyes stared right at her, the tiny mouth working an invisible pacifier.

Yelena studied Bella as she gurgled, her gummy grin stretching. Yet she couldn't squash the trepidation fluttering around in her belly.

Alex was a smart man: once he saw Bella he'd do the math.

There'd be no going back. Yet leaving Bella at home was not an option. Her childhood, all those years of emotional neglect, had seen to that.

"If Alex Rush wants me, then he'll have to deal with you too, sweetheart."

You can do this. She put entirely too much emphasis on what she'd meant to Alex. He'd moved on from what they'd been to each other, just as she had. He didn't care enough to hate her. What mattered now—what had always mattered— was doing her job. Turning the tide of public opinion was his sole purpose. Whatever he felt about her would only be temporary, just as this campaign was.

Alex settled into the luxurious comfort of Rush Airline's private Cessna, trying to focus on the work spread in front of him but failing.

His grievances against Yelena's brother had been gathering momentum ever since his father's accidental-death ruling. Alex had left the sanctuary of Diamond Bay in June, returning to Canberra to discover the huge ripple effect William Rush's death had wrought. The speculation, the unrelenting police interrogation and the intense press scrutiny paled in comparison to discovering Carlos's true colors.

He muttered a foul oath, the blade of betrayal still sharp. Carlos had been a casual acquaintance from university, one who'd mixed in the same elite social circles. On a whim he'd considered Carlos's business proposal, encouraged by the prospect of escaping from the shadow of Australia's favorite son, William Rush.

Two short years later and he and Carlos had set up a partnership, developing a handful of franchised travel agencies under the name of Sprint Travel.

He wasn't so blind to ignore the fact that Yelena's approval had played a part in his decision. Hell, he could still hear her glowing endorsement of her brother as partner material.

That woman could tempt the Lord himself…even if she were sister to the Devil.

He dragged a hand over his jaw and absently rubbed the whisper of stubble, its familiar rasp an empty echo in the cabin.

You were an idiot. A stupid, bloody idiot, thinking with your libido, not your head.

All his life he'd had this unnerving ability to know when people weren't telling the whole truth—his father had crudely dubbed it "Alex's crap detector" with a certain amount of pride. But with Carlos he hadn't seen it coming…and yeah, he thought grudgingly, not *wanted* to see it because the brother of Gabriela and Yelena Valero couldn't possibly be a lying snake…right?

He snorted. Wrong on all counts. A week after he'd been cleared of his father's death, he'd been served with the breach of contract documents. He'd read them through, choking back his shock at the neatly typed legalese. If the courts sided with Carlos and the partnership was dissolved, all Alex's shares would go to Carlos. Technically it was legal, but morally?

Before he had time to wrap his head around that, the next blow fell. A loyal agency manager with friends at the Federal Police and the Canberra Times had voiced concerns about Carlos's creative accountancy practices.

And that's when things had turned ugly.

The betrayal wounded him deep, much deeper than any financial loss. With fury in his blood, fueling every waking hour, he'd dug for the truth. And as the articles about his family steadily grew worse, so, too, did his desire for vengeance. He'd used every contact, every favor at his disposal to uncover something, anything solid to wield as his sword of justice, but until recently Carlos had been clever. No paper trail and no one willing to go on record.

And then, suddenly, two breakthroughs. Last week he'd contacted three potential victims of Carlos's rip-off schemes who hadn't automatically slammed the door in his face. And, more importantly, Alex had discovered Carlos was the one who'd been feeding infidelity stories of his dead father to the press since March.

Everything had clicked into horrible focus. Yelena was the only person who could've overheard that shameful, ugly confrontation with his father in his office. The only one who could've blabbed to Carlos about it.

It wasn't about business anymore. This was personal.

Damn them. Damn *her*.

His fist tightened on his pen until a tiny cracking noise forced him to release it with a hollow clatter. The marks across his palm rose quickly.

Soon they would be on their way to Diamond Bay, where he'd have Yelena completely to himself. He'd make sure Carlos Valero knew his perfect, respectable sister had willingly fallen into his bed then he'd hand all his evidence about Carlos's wrongdoing over to the authorities. Only complete and utter humiliation would vindicate him.

Wasn't one sister enough for you? Keep your hands off Yelena or God help you, I'll bring you down. His mouth slashed into a grim smile as he remembered Carlos's hollow phone threat, now securely saved on his message bank.

Anger meant mistakes and Alex was counting on Carlos to make one.

Alex glanced at his shiny Tag Hauer. What if she didn't show? He tossed away that thought as quickly as it formed. He knew Yelena, knew how hard she worked to control her world, how she craved independence and respect. A successful campaign with the Rush name behind it would send her career into orbit.

Yet relief still surprised him when he finally heard her voice in the alcove.

Then she rounded the corner carrying a strangely shaped bundle and he frowned.

"What's that?" he asked over the sudden roar of the plane's engines.

"'That' is my daughter."

Oblivious to Alex's stunned silence, she smiled at the attendant who'd flipped down the bulkhead's portable cot then gently placed the bundle inside.

"You don't have a baby," he said sharply as she eased into the seat opposite.

"I do." She shrugged off her jacket then buckled up, keeping her eyes firmly on her task. "Her name is Bella."

"You adopted."

His tight statement snapped her eyes to his. "That's none of your business, Alex."

"It is if you're bringing your private life to work."

Her icy gaze matched his. "You of all people can understand why she's here. I will not hand her over to my family while I run off for a week, no matter how badly I need your account."

Her steady glare, her steely posture, all spoke of complete and utter control.

He paused, recalling her proud, dry-eyed confession that the Valero children had been raised by nannies and boarding schools while Maria Valero had played the part of the foreign diplomat's wife to perfectly coiffed perfection.

It had been the first time he'd been aware of something more than just physical desire for Yelena.

His teeth ground together with an inward growl. "So she's yours?"

In her infinitesimal pause he had his answer. He didn't need to see the quickly suppressed anxiety in her eyes that accompanied the curt nod.

A child. Yelena's child.

How had he missed *that*?

A deathly calm swept in to cleave his entire body, slicing at his control and reopening past wounds all over again.

"How old?" he got out.

She actually had the audacity to lift that proud chin of hers, to meet his glare with one of her own. "Five months."

As he did the math then double-checked, a thin film of rage clouded his vision, choking him into silence. If he'd had any smidgen of doubt about his plans, any tiny attack of conscience, she'd well and truly obliterated them.

The night Yelena had declared she'd loved him, the night of his father's death, she'd been pregnant with another man's child.

Three

The plane banked high in the air then slowly eased off. For the next hour, Yelena tried to bury herself in Alex's clippings, but time and again she caught herself staring out the window, into the painfully bright clouds and searing blue sky.

Bella finally stirred and she gave up any pretense of working. Instead she rummaged in her bag for a bottle of formula. But even as she fed Bella, she was acutely aware of the man seated directly opposite…and his complete and utter lack of interest in her. When Bella began to fidget—obviously sensing her mother's tension—Yelena glanced over.

The dark scowl as he focused on the papers on the table was so oddly out of place that her eyes lingered. She'd never seen Alex so angry, so untouchable. Her memories of him were scattered with flirtatious banter and unspoken attraction.

Don't forget kisses. Treacherous kisses that promised as much as they cajoled her to forget.

She glanced down at Bella, at those large half-mast eyes,

her mouth hanging slack on the bottle. With a tender smile, she put a towel on her shoulder then placed the baby over.

Ten minutes later, she moved her sleeping daughter back to the cot, packed away the forgotten paperwork then focused on the land spread out below.

Mile upon mile of red sand, punctuated by a hint of scrub. With most of Australia still in the throes of waning winter, August in outback Northern Territory meant rolling hot sand dunes, coupled with freezing cold nights.

She'd looked up the National Bureau of Meteorology on the Internet while waiting for Alex's car service and stumbled across a real-time Web site that beamed Ayers Rock, Diamond Bay Resort and the Yandurruh community to the entire world.

Gabriela had mentioned the resort once but her bare-bones description didn't do the stunning Internet feed justice. And now, looming in the distance, Yelena could just make out the shiny, curved dips and arches of Australia's most exclusive resort.

Perched on the edge of sacred Aboriginal land that included distinctive Ayers Rock, she'd expected Diamond Bay to be a towering eyesore in comparison to the Outback's raw beauty. But instead of a monstrosity, the resort was more like an undulating oasis. As the plane took a pass then looped back around to the small airstrip, Yelena unashamedly pressed her nose up against the cold glass. The structure flowed across the land, shimmering in the midday sun, the elegant, curving roofs rolling gently like an enormous albatross flying low across the stark red desert that stretched far into the distance.

Tension momentarily forgotten, she turned to Alex.

"What made your father build such a lavish resort way out here?"

Slowly, almost reluctantly, he raised his gaze from his papers to meet her eyes. "For privacy. And solitude." Then he turned back to his work, dismissing her.

Yelena inwardly cringed at his polite response, stripped of any inflection.

Was it so difficult to look at her, to talk to her? An unwelcome tangle of regret stuck in her throat and Yelena swallowed, forcing it down.

Thankfully, the awful silence was drowned out by the mechanics of the landing plane, then the clunk of doors and whirr of steps.

As she grabbed her jacket then reached for Bella, she felt Alex's presence close behind. When she turned, she saw her briefcase in his hand. With a spare silent nod, he indicated she should precede him.

Murmuring her thanks, she took the metal steps one slow clink at a time, keenly aware of Alex following, watching her every step.

A long, black limousine met them at the airstrip, and as Alex silently held the door open for her, Yelena noticed the baby capsule in the backseat.

She strapped a gurgling Bella down and got in, leaving Alex the window. When the door closed with a solid thunk, sealing them off in air-conditioned comfort sudden claustrophobia from the familiar spacious luxury made her breath catch. It had everything to do with the man who sat broodingly beside her, giving her the cold shoulder as if she'd committed an unforgivable sin.

With a sad sigh, she tilted her body away from him and murmured soft nothings at her daughter, making smiley faces as she quickly glanced at her watch.

Six days, twelve hours to go.

She placed a hand on Bella's little kicking feet, tension sending her stomach into a hundred fluttery butterflies.

This was ridiculous. Resolutely she pulled her back straight and turned in her seat, giving Alex her full attention.

"What do you want to achieve from this campaign?"

Visibly startled, he turned from the window, his expression dark as thunder. Yet he remained silent.

"Alex?" She prompted. "Your goals?"

"Who's the father?"

She recoiled. "That's none of your business!"

"Like hell it's not."

"Like hell it is!" Fury boiled up, singeing her control. "We are over, Alex. You and I have a business relationship, nothing more. I don't discuss my private life with clients and I don't intend to start now."

"And yet you bring your daughter on a business trip."

Her eyes narrowed. "This is the first time a client has made unreasonable demands. You left me no choice."

"Everyone always has a choice, Yelena."

She stiffened but refused to bite. "If you're concerned about not having my full attention, I can assure you Bella will in no way inhibit my ability to do my job."

"I see." His stare felt like smoldering flames on Yelena's skin. Fury, yes, but also a sliver of something else. Pride? Pain?

No. Alex Rush would never show that type of vulnerability.

A hard knot twisted inside her. For a second, she thought she'd seen something more beneath that hostile surface. The way he held his body, the tight line of his jaw, the flinty eyes, all convinced her of that.

Once upon a time they'd been friends. She should be relieved he'd managed to clamp a lid on his emotions, yet all she felt was cheated somehow.

"I can't offer you anything, Alex, except my full and utter focus on your campaign. Please respect that." *I can't erase what you see as a painful betrayal.* Instead she gathered up her self-control and forged on. "Now. Tell me about your goals for this campaign."

He glared at her, almost disbelieving, until suddenly, something cold and distant swept over him.

He glanced away, too nonchalant to be convincing. "For months the papers have been peddling lies and gossip about my father having an affair."

Yelena nodded. "I read the clippings. How's that affected your mother and sister?"

"My mother was politely asked to leave two of her charity boards. Instead of the usual phone calls, invitations and appearance requests, there's been a thunderous silence. And Chelsea's tennis trials sponsor pulled out which, before you ask, isn't about the money—it's about the stamp of approval being withdrawn on the basis of a bunch of lies."

"And, of course, your father isn't around to defend himself."

He gave her a sharp, unreadable look. "Of course," he echoed.

"Alex…" She chewed on the inside of her cheek for a second. "*Was* your father cheating?"

A sudden scowl creased his forehead. "No."

He paused as if about to add more, but when silence followed she asked slowly, "Can you be a hundred percent sure?"

"Of course I can't—no one can!"

"Okay." She ignored his hot glare and continued. "So we need to refocus, attract positive attention. An effective campaign is about subtlety—we want to create a slow but steady groundswell of public support without being blatant."

"If you're thinking of going down that clichéd, 'bring out the loving family for the press conference' route—"

Her mouth twisted. "No, I'll leave that to our next disgraced politician. It's a well-used tactic but it does evoke remorse and sympathy—you know, the whole 'he loves his family so he must be a good guy' thing. But it has to be done right. Tell me, while we're on the topic of your father, did you ever issue a public statement declaring your innocence in his death?"

"My solicitor did."

"But did *you,* personally?"

"No."

"Why not?"

"Because…" He frowned. "I was never charged. The police investigation was a complete farce, based on anonymous tips and half-baked rumors. I didn't want to give it more attention."

"I see."

"No, you don't." He met her gaze stonily. "After my father died, there was an almighty outpouring of public sympathy. The great and brilliant William Rush, taken in his prime. It went on for weeks—his brutal childhood and meteoric rise from poverty, his business dealings, influential friends. Then when I was dragged in for questioning, his fondness for gambling and drinking started making headlines."

"That's when it turned."

"Exactly. The cheating rumors were the last straw. My mother doesn't deserve that kind of smear. Nor does Chelsea." His eyes suddenly sparked, burning with purpose. "You asked me what I want from this campaign? I want my family to be accepted on their own achievements, not judged based on malicious gossip. I want you to woo the press, the public and their peers. And I want you to do it with subtlety."

"I'm always discreet."

"No. I mean, as far as everyone is concerned, I am not your client. And you are not running my PR campaign. I don't want to give the press any cynical 'stage-managed spin' headlines."

"I see," she said, frowning, not seeing at all. "So how do you intend to explain my presence?"

Alex's brief scrutiny said much more than his casual shrug. "Old friends catching up?"

Yelena's stomach pitched as the car pulled smoothly to a stop. Flustered, she shoved her bag strap over her shoulder and began to unclip Bella. "Who's going to believe that?"

"They believed all that crap about my father, didn't they?"

Yelena gently lifted the sleeping baby then got out of the limo. "Why on earth would I—" The words died on her tongue as she straightened, her cursory glance transforming into a wide-eyed stare.

She gulped. This place wasn't five-star—it was a hundred. From the ground, the resort's magnificence couldn't be more obvious. The frontage was old-style Grecian villa, with twin marble entry columns, sky-blue tiles and sky-high ceilings. Yet the apartments that rose on either side screamed sleek sophistication. The unusual rolling-roof design was stunning, the white-and-blue tiles complementing the stark desert surroundings.

"Takes your breath away, doesn't it?"

Yelena turned back to Alex, who was leaning against the car door with crossed arms and ankles, a powerful, commanding figure in brooding silence.

Ouch. The snapshot moment tightened her chest in painful remembrance. Last year, the same man but with a come-hither smile. She'd been leaving work, only to find him leaning nonchalantly on her car. Then he'd reached out and kissed her until her knees gave way...

All she could do was nod and slip her sunglasses up her nose. "Gabriela said the place was huge but..."

His blink-and-you'd-miss-it frown forced her words back down her throat.

"It was designed by Tom Wright, the guy who did Dubai's Burj Al Arab." His response was cool and impersonal, setting her teeth on edge. "I'll show you to your room." He nodded to the steward, who had their bags in hand, then strode into the marble-columned entrance without waiting to see if she would follow.

Before his long-legged strides took him to the far wall of his suite, Alex spun around and resumed pacing, raking a hand through his hair. He scrubbed at the roots, recalling that brief conversation in the car.

He'd known Yelena for nearly fifteen years, a good part of those spent lusting after her in typical adolescent fantasy. But he'd never, ever thought her capable of deliberate deceit. Until now.

Was your father cheating?

Why had she asked when she damn well knew the answer? She'd overheard his argument with his father, and hadn't hesitated to share what she knew with Carlos.

He reached the wall again and with a curse and a growl, turned.

She was trying to throw him, to make out she was innocent. That had to be it. Yet...

There'd been a small hesitancy in her question, a flush to her cheeks. The way her dark eyes briefly met his then flitted away.

He ground to a halt, a foot away from the sleek, monochrome writing desk. Carlos's betrayal had seriously screwed up his mind, made him doubt himself for the first time since...

He snapped his head up, glaring at his reflection in the golden mirror above the desk. Thanks to that one mistake, he'd spent the past months revisiting every deal, every business choice he'd made. More bloody time wasted on second-guessing perfectly legitimate decisions.

With an angry sigh he yanked his tie loose and undid the top buttons of his shirt.

It would drive him crazy if he let it. He'd already allowed

sentiment to seep in, putting him two steps back with Yelena.

Way to start the big seduction, mate. Yet he couldn't stop the questions from tumbling out, the need to know overriding all common sense. Yelena always had that effect on him. Twice he'd let anger rule the moment and twice she'd slammed up the shield, using their business relationship as defense. If he kept pissing her off, he'd have a better chance of harnessing a bushfire than getting her into bed. It was time to refocus on his plan.

Just like that his brain emptied, Yelena's features charging into the void to hijack his senses. *Finally,* his body seemed to groan. *You've caught up.*

It'd been too long since her subtle, exotic scent had sent him into meltdown, since he'd felt the silken slide of that wild chocolate hair against his skin.

And another man had claimed that right.

No. A bolt of fury jerked his jaw into a clench, unable to stop his mind from going there.

It could have been your child. Yours and Yelena's.

With gritted teeth he forced himself to let it go. And if his father hadn't been drunk and drowned in their pool, this alternate reality would cease to exist. But he *had* and now Alex had to deal with everything stemming from that one life-changing event.

If he couldn't get a grip, then his plans were history. Which left his family with nothing but a legacy of scandal and lies, terrible reminders of a past that he'd vowed would be buried with his tyrant father.

He glared out the large glass doors, out onto the wild beauty of the Australian Outback. To his far left, the distinctive ochre of Ayers Rock loomed, a sharp contrast to the overt lushness of Diamond Bay.

He loved the peace and isolation of this place. It was the only one of William's creations that didn't scream his autocratic presence in every brick and line, the only place untainted by his violence.

Alex absently rubbed a palm across his shoulder, recalling old wounds. He'd regularly endured the man's fists and his "fight for what you want—no one else will" dictum, a dictum that had surprisingly stuck. The only thing of value he'd gotten from that son of a bitch.

It was time to get his head straight and see this thing through.

The memory of soft eyes and a sinful laugh washed over him, making him groan. That thought carried him out the door, down the heavily carpeted gold-and-cream hallway to the end of the corridor where he'd deliberately placed Yelena.

He knocked and after a muffled "Hang on!" Yelena opened the door with a rushed smile. Her expression faded when she saw him standing there.

She'd removed her business suit. Instead, she was dressed in jeans and a stark white T-shirt, the dark denim a perfect frame for her long legs, the soft cotton shirt clinging demurely to her curves and prodding his imagination into overdrive. Extreme womanly curves.

He offered a thousand colorful curses to his growing libido before she silently stepped aside to let him enter.

"Did Jasmine come and see you?" he asked by way of greeting before striding into the room.

Yelena's mind blanked as an unexpected tingle flushed her skin, his warm body and familiar scent brushing fleetingly past.

"The babysitter," he reminded her.

She gave herself a mental shake. "Yes, she's in the bedroom with Bella. Thank you for arranging that."

He shrugged then paused in the middle of the room, surveying it. "The resort provides an exceptional nanny service. Is the room to your liking?"

"Perfect—if a bit large."

"All our suites come with a living area, two bedrooms, separate bathroom. And of course, a view."

He picked up a remote control from the coffee table and thumbed a button.

Slowly, the curtains began to whir apart.

"Your curtains are electronic?" she asked.

"Yeah." Her surprise amused him: the small grin he gave had her cool resolve thawing an inch. "Can't have our guests *manually* opening their curtains."

She shook her head, reluctantly matching his smile. "Of course not. They might—oh."

It was a fantasy view. Dead ahead, a huge cliff face loomed, a waterfall glinting in the sun as it crashed over the edge into a massive lagoon. A veritable forest of native flora gathered at the base, creating a protective canopy that shaded a paved walkway. Yelena could barely pick out the private cabanas Diamond Bay provided for all its pool goers.

It was like something from a big-budget movie set where the characters stumbled upon a fertile, ancient land miles below the earth's surface. Yet Yelena knew it was the real thing. Diamond Bay—the only man-made body of water in the state.

And surrounding it all, the shiny curves of the resort gently undulated, forming a completely decadent—and totally private—haven.

"That's…"

"Amazing?"

Yelena took one step towards the view, then another. "Breathtaking."

He crossed his arms. "William Rush did have a taste for the spectacular."

She slowly swung her gaze to him, studying his profile as he stared out at the view.

Something was off. There was tension, yes. She'd expected

that—even disgust, considering what she'd dumped on him in the plane. But there was something more… She grazed her eyes over his face. The almost imperceptible frown creasing his brow. The strong, fixed jaw. The aquiline slope of his nose that led down to a mouth that she remembered was way too warm, way too tempting.

He shifted, those azure eyes snaring her. "I had a feeling you'd like it," he murmured, almost to himself.

A spark of something deep within flared her senses for one second, but in the next he glanced away and she wondered if she'd just imagined it.

It left her breathless. And irritated.

"I'll show you where you'll be working," he said shortly, completely unaware of his effect on her heart rate.

She nodded, disappeared into the bedroom then returned with her briefcase and a thick notepad.

"Your sister's fourteen, correct?" Yelena began as they made their way from the suite and down the hushed hall.

"Fifteen in March." His eyes suddenly relaxed. "You've never met her, have you?"

"Once. Gabriela invited her to a thing at the embassy last year."

"Ah, that's right… the Christmas in July Ball." They turned left and stopped at the elevator bay. "She was stoked. Couldn't stop flashing that 'special guest' invitation under everyone's nose." His mouth quirked as he punched the button.

"Your mother couldn't come that night—she was sick, right?"

"Yeah." His eyelids suddenly came down as he crossed his arms, angling his body towards the elevators.

Odd. Yelena frowned but before she could add anything more, Alex spoke, his gaze still on the closed elevator doors.

"That was the night you kissed me for the first time. In the kitchen, remember?"

She snapped her eyes up, cheeks warm. "*You* kissed *me*."

His mouth slanted. "And you told me to take a hike afterwards."

"You were Gabriela's boyfriend."

"Only one of many."

"Are you accusing my sister of—"

"Oh, come off it, Yelena." She just caught his eye roll before the doors pinged open. "You and I both know Gabriela's a good-time girl in every sense of the word. I served as her designated arm decoration when she was in town but I certainly wasn't her only love interest."

I can't talk about this. Yelena tightened her grip on her bag, steadfastly focusing on the closing elevator doors as the memories flushed over her skin, making her tingle.

"Tell me more about Chelsea."

He paused, letting her know he knew she was changing the subject. Finally, he said, "She's an amazing kid—a promising tennis player, too. Brash and tough on the outside but inside…"

"A typical teenager—vulnerable and unsure."

"Yeah." He looked at Yelena then, his small smile startling her. "What would you know about that?"

"Everything." Alex watched her mouth twitch as they both left the elevator and headed across the marble lobby. "I was the new kid at school, remember? And a foreigner."

"I remember your first day." How could he forget? She'd been every male senior's wet dream—a stunning, dark-haired beauty driving up to Radford College in a sleek black BMW, hair blowing, fashionably impassive behind flashy Dior sunglasses.

"I was nervous as hell," she said, snapping him from his fantasy as they kept walking past the reception area.

"Couldn't tell. You glided through that car park like you owned the place."

Yelena gave a short laugh as he held open a set of glass doors for her. "'Glided'? Hardly."

"Yeah. Gabriela bounces through life. You glide like a perfectly groomed ship on smooth water." Palm down, he cut his hand through the air, a visual to back up his statement.

"Is that how you see me—perfect? Untouchable?"

He paused, his hand on the door that proclaimed, simply, Alexander Rush. She watched his sensual mouth curve, his piercing blue eyes creasing in sudden humor.

"Never untouchable, Yelena."

Her breath caught as she remained trapped in the steady knowledge of his gaze. *This* was the Alex she knew—the teasing charmer who threw out little double entendres just to see her fluster. Not the bitter man flinging accusations in her office. And certainly not the Alex of the dark moments, the hidden secrets and brooding silences she'd thought Gabriela had exaggerated for dramatic effect.

"Coffee?"

"What?"

"I said, do you want coffee?" His mouth tweaked into a delicious grin. "We can have it out by the pool."

Guiltily she nodded. She'd known her sister and Alex were a mismatch the instant Gabriela had told her…when? May. Over a year ago. A lifetime. Yet she'd loved him in her own way. Didn't he deserve to know what had happened?

As she stood in the still expanse of Alex's office, pretending to take in her surroundings while he made a phone call, she wrestled with the promise her parents had wrenched from her. Finally he hung up.

"My mother and Chelsea will meet us at Ruby's—one of our many coffee bars—at four."

"Alex…"

"Yes?" He placed his hands on his hips, head tilted in familiar awareness.

Gabriela's dead. It was right on the tip of her tongue, sitting there all ready to come out, but with one gulp she swallowed it. She'd been clear with Alex from the start—she was here for business. Disturbed at how easy her control had slipped in less than a day, she quickly grabbed for the reins.

"Do your mother and sister know why I'm here?" she asked.

Slowly he leaned against his desk, bracing his palms on the rich, dark wood.

"No. And I don't want them to, at least not yet. My mother will think it's unnecessary…that British stiff-upper-lip reserve thing. She'd say I was wasting my money and your time, that everything would eventually blow over—" He stopped midsentence, his jaw tightening. Then he cleared his throat, crossed his arms and said, "They've been here two weeks and only just started to relax—I want to keep it that way."

His pointed look stung. "I know how to do my job."

"Good." He nodded to the huge aerial shot of Diamond Bay on the wall opposite. "People pay for a media-free zone here. No papers, TV, phone, Internet—unless by request. I've given you a conference room next door with everything you need. Only guests are allowed into the resort, and only then by private plane, so no reporters. You'll have complete privacy to work."

Complete privacy. In a stunning resort that radiated Alex's presence and family power from every floor, every wall. Yet despite the tension rumbling between them like an ominous earthquake warning, she'd felt a connection to this place from the moment she'd set foot on the rich red soil. As if the sole purpose of her stay was to help her relax.

"Do you get to stay here often?"

He paused. "Not as much as I'd like. I travel between Sydney, Canberra, L.A. and London, mostly."

Yelena tipped her head. "London? So Sprint Travel is thinking of franchising to the U.K.? Carlos…"

Yelena let her words peter out at Alex's tight face. "Carlos what?"

"He…he just mentioned it in passing."

"I see," he said smoothly, before straightening to his full six-foot-three height. "But to answer—no. Rush Airlines has investments in the U.K. and the States. Do you want to see your work space?"

He quickly left the office and walked down the hall, leaving Yelena no choice but to follow.

Four

"Welcome to Diamond Falls, Yelena." Pamela Rush's handshake might have been hesitant but her smile was sincerely warm. A pair of flowing beige pants and a floral shirt tied low around her middle emphasized a trim figure, with a large broad-brimmed sun hat completing the ensemble.

"My gardening clothes," Pam said with a smile, then swept off her hat and gave her short, choppy hair a ruffle. "I have a greenhouse extended onto my suite. We try to be as self-sufficient as we can."

Yelena noticed the loving smile Pam gave Alex as he sat down. Then she glanced over at the lanky girl—Alex's sister—who was lounging unceremoniously in the comfy sofa chair opposite.

"I already ordered coffee for us—I hope you don't mind." A tinge of worry lit Pam's eyes. "Unless you drink tea, Yelena…?"

Yelena smiled reassuringly. "Couldn't function without my coffee."

"You're Gabriela's sister, right?" Chelsea asked as she swung her legs around, her feet landing with a small thunk on the slate floor. The teenager was all long limbs and coltish grace in cutoff denim shorts and black T-shirt declaring Vampire Princess in blood red. Familiar white iPod headphones dangled from her neck, her brown hair pulled up into a ponytail, revealing a makeup-free face. She looked all of ten years old.

"I am," Yelena said. "You and I met last year."

"At the Christmas in July Ball." Chelsea grinned and nodded. "You were dressed in black Colette Dinnigan—from her *next* season winter collection."

Yelena smiled. "I have friends in high places. And you have a good memory. Are you interested in fashion?"

Chelsea shrugged. "Sort of."

"One of her many interests," Pamela Rush said with a gentle smile at her daughter. Chelsea blinked and shrugged, trying to carry off teenage blasé but losing. The intelligence in her blue eyes, so like Alex's, indicated much more depth than Yelena suspected people knew. "Chelsea's going to be the next Martina," Pam added proudly.

"Mum!" Chelsea rolled her eyes as she wrapped her headphones around the iPod. "Don't—"

"Excuse me, Mr. Rush. Drinks?"

The waiter placed three coffees and a thick chocolate shake before them with a flourish. Yelena caught Chelsea's flushed gaze as it flitted up to the cute waiter then back to the tabletop.

Smothering a smile, she turned her attention to Alex's mother.

She'd seen photos of Pamela Rush in the gossip magazines and society pages. The former airline hostess had aged well, with hardly a wrinkle on her striking face, no visible grey hairs in her rich, brown pixie cut.

"Didn't you have long hair at one point?" Yelena asked curiously.

If she hadn't been studying the woman so closely, she would've missed the slight waver on Pam's lips just before they stretched into a smile.

"Sometimes you just need a change."

Yelena nodded, glancing away to cover up her embarrassment. Of course. The woman had lost a husband, her son had been accused of murder. Some people ran away, some drank. Some simply went to pieces. Pamela Rush cut her hair.

"So what brings you to Diamond Bay, Yelena?" Pam asked.

Yelena gave Alex a fleeting glance. He raised one eyebrow, inviting her to continue.

"Distraction-free work—"

"And a little relaxation, too." Alex added evenly, his smile sending a quiver of warmth into her limbs.

"Well, this is the place for it," Pam said with a nod.

As Pam poured milk into her coffee, Yelena made a few observations. *Genuine smile. Polite. Poised.* Her fingers twitched, eager to make notes, but knew she'd have to wait until later. Instead she picked up a packet of sugar, gave it a flick then ripped open the top and dumped the contents into her black coffee.

She lowered her eyes to furtively study Alex. He appeared calm, the muscles in his face relaxed, his brow smooth. She even caught a small twitch of approval lingering at the corner of his mouth.

A frisson of pleasure jetted through her body, startling her. *This isn't your first campaign. You can't let a client's stamp of approval go to your head.*

"Is Gabriela overseas?" Chelsea said suddenly, leaning forward with her elbows on her knees.

Thrown, Yelena slowly took her cup and raised it to her lips before focusing her attention on the teenager. "Um… yes."

"For the fashion season? It starts in September, right, with New York, then London, Milan and Paris?"

It was only after Yelena had taken a sip of scalding coffee and returned the cup to the saucer that she realized her other hand had been halfway up to her necklace. Instinctively her eyes met Alex's. At his frown, she lowered her hand then clasped them together on the table.

"How do you know?" She gave Chelsea a small, curious smile. "Gabriela wasn't—" she paused to swallow, then finished faintly "—she hasn't modeled for years."

"I know—she's a booker for Cat Walker Models in Sydney, right? I've been following their blog. They said they were going to send staff to cover the shows and I just figured she'd be the obvious choice."

The dull pain squeezed her heart but she managed to return Chelsea's smile. "I think you're more than 'sort of' interested in fashion."

"Yeah," she muttered and glanced away with a barely hidden grimace. When she returned her gaze to Yelena's, it was…different. Hard. As if she'd aged ten years in the space of two seconds. "But Dad reckoned it was a waste of time."

Then she reached for her shake and began to vigorously stir it with the straw.

What on earth was that? Yelena chanced another look at Alex while everyone drank but failed to glean anything from his controlled blue stare.

Too controlled. Yelena dropped her eyes as her thoughts began to snowball. What was going on here? She cast her mind back to this morning, rehashing their conversations. Yet she couldn't pin down anything tangible, any dead giveaway that would assuage her concerns. It was more a gut feeling, something instinctive that told her Alex wasn't telling her everything. After months—years—of covert flirting and casual chat during endless social functions they'd been thrown into, she could sense it. She could sense it every time the topic of conversation turned to his family. And she could sense it after three clandestine moments when they'd shared fevered kisses and whispers of hot passion.

She knew it now.

In one of Gabriela's rare moments of insight, her sister had likened Alex Rush to a dormant volcano—beautiful and calm on the outside, but inside a raging mass of hot, bubbling conflict.

Take care of him, Yelena. He's one of the good guys.

Yelena glared at her cup. Damn it. She'd been trying to erase Gabriela's gentle command from her memory, just as she'd been forcing herself not to think about Alex and all the complexities that made him tick. But she was involved again—and it didn't only include him now.

With sudden inspiration, Yelena placed her spoon on her saucer and leaned forward. "I tell you what, Chelsea. I know a few people in Sydney—if you're interested, I can get us front-row tickets to David Jones's fashion show next month."

Chelsea's rounded eyes snapped up to hers. "Really?"

When she glanced over at Pam, Yelena quickly added, "Of course, your mum would have to approve."

"Mum? Please? Please, please, pleeeeeease?"

But it was Alex who butted in with, "What about your training? And school?"

The spark of defiance in the teenager's eyes was hard to miss. "What about it?"

Pam began awkwardly, "I thought you were focusing on the Perth trials next year?"

Chelsea glared at the tabletop, muttering something under her breath.

"What?" Alex said with a frown.

"I said, 'I doubt I'd get in, anyway.'"

"So you want to just drop it? Is—" Alex paused then

leaned forward in his chair, irritation evident "—is that what you want? After you've spent so much time and effort on training?"

Chelsea's expression turned sullen. "Why don't you start yelling about how you've spent thousands on my tennis career? Then you'd *really* sound like Dad."

If Chelsea had picked up her soda spoon and stabbed him with it, Alex couldn't have looked more hurt.

"Sweetheart…" Pam said slowly before Chelsea cut her off with a venomous look.

Wow. Anger like that didn't come from just a little family disagreement. Fascinated yet discomfited, Yelena watched the scenario play out before her, unable to look away.

"If you want something that badly—" Pam began.

Chelsea leaped to her feet, face flushed. "Don't you *dare* quote Dad to me, not now, not after—"

"Chelsea!" Alex said roughly.

She scowled at him. "And you shouldn't be defending him! This whole thing sucks! Everything sucks!"

And with that, she stormed across the café and out the glass doors.

Alex scraped his chair back but Pam put a hand on his arm, shaking her head. He sat, his face turbulent, as an awkward silence fell.

Yelena looked over to Pam, who was making short work of the napkin in her lap, eyes staring at her half-empty coffee. And Alex, well, that gaze would end up burning a hole in the table pretty soon.

"You know what?" Yelena said firmly, turning to Pam. "I'd love to see your greenhouse if you have the time."

The older woman glanced up, blinking rapidly. "Now?"

"Sure." She tempered her request with a smile. "Work can wait. And I love plants even though I have a black thumb."

"Black thumb?"

"They always end up withering away, despite my best efforts."

Pam's shaky smile told Yelena she was grateful for the attention shift, yet Alex's expression remained closed.

Yelena stood and casually linked her arm through the older woman's. But then, suddenly, she paused with a confused blink. Had Pamela Rush *flinched?* Her eyes sought Pam's but their crystal-blue depths reflected nothing but gentle politeness.

She shook herself, dismissing the moment.

"I'll see you for dinner, darling?" Pam said, glancing back to Alex.

Yelena didn't want to look at him but she managed to force her gaze to where he still sat, silent and thoughtful.

When he looked first at his mother, then her, she could see the wheels of his mind working overtime. With one raised eyebrow, she met his eyes steadily.

He glanced back to Pam. "I'll probably be working. I'll let you know." Slowly he added, "What about Chelsea?"

Pam shook her head. "She's been angry for the last two weeks. I've been giving her some space, so please don't chase her down. She needs to—" she paused, as if rethinking the words "—figure out who she is and what she wants. You know what it's like at that age."

"Yeah."

Yelena couldn't fail to notice Alex's parting scowl, dark with something she couldn't quite put her finger on. It lingered in her mind long after Pam led her from the café, across the foyer and towards the private suites.

Alex was neck-deep in numbers with only half his mind on the task when Yelena breezed into his office an hour later. "You have to tell your mother."

He slowly placed his Montblanc pen on the sheaf of

notes and leaned back. The leather chair gently groaned in protest.

"What have you said to her?"

"Nothing." She put her hands on her hips, obviously unaware how that emphasized the generous flare of her curves. "But I've never worked on a campaign that didn't have the full support of the client."

"*I'm* your client."

She shifted her weight, one long leg thrust forward aggressively, tilting those hips in one slow, suggestive motion. Alex's breath caught in sharp appreciation.

"Tell me, if it weren't for Pam and Chelsea, would you have hired me?" Yelena said.

If it weren't for Carlos they both wouldn't be here. "No," he said curtly, arousal doused as resentment began to bubble up inside. He swiftly stood. "What have you two been talking about?"

"Well, naturally she asked what I did for a living so pretty soon she'll put two and two together." She paused, shaking her head. Alex watched a small strand of hair escape her ponytail and settle on her shoulder. With an impatient sweep, she shoved it back.

"I also get the feeling she thinks you and I are—" she paused, her hand fluttering up to her necklace "—conducting some kind of secret liaison."

"I see."

When he moved out from behind his desk, Alex noticed the way she put weight onto her back foot, unsure and unsteady. As if poised for a quick exit.

Yelena never backed down from an argument. Which meant something else had unnerved her, something that went beyond mere discomfort at his mother's assumptions. Was he finally getting to her? Just as satisfaction curled his mouth into a grin, a dark alternate thought thinned it.

"Being romantically linked with a suspected murderer embarrasses you."

Yelena eyes widened at the hint of disgust peppering his flat statement. "No! How could you possibly think that?"

"So what's the problem?"

"You have to stop lying to her."

His eyes narrowed. "I am not lying."

She snorted, unperturbed by his mounting irritation. "Lying by omission is still lying. I get enough of that from my bro—"

Appalled, she snapped her mouth shut...not quick enough.

"What's Carlos done?" He growled.

What on earth was she thinking? Their eyes deadlocked, both unwilling to back down until Yelena finally conceded.

"Nothing. He's said absolutely nothing to me for months. This whole silent treatment you're giving him isn't going to solve the problem, you know."

"What makes you think there's a problem?"

"Do not treat me like an idiot, Alex. There's a problem."

Instantly, the temperature dropped. "That's none of your business."

"Rubbish. Not only will this impact on Sprint Travel and this campaign, but he's my brother—your business partner."

He shot her a look. "What happened to your 'no personal questions' rule?" He slowly crossed his arms. "Can't have it both ways. Or—" he let the words trail off, one eyebrow raised "—are you deliberately trying to pick a fight?"

His voice dipped into a shockingly intimate timbre. Immediately her body started to tingle with anticipation, heart rate thumping.

His mouth tweaked. "You always loved a good, long—"

"Alex!"

"Argument." Now he was grinning at her outright. They were having a serious discussion and he was *amused?*

Infuriated, she tried to pull herself together. "Maybe I'm getting sick and tired of all your weird looks."

"What weird looks?"

"As if you can't stand me one moment but the next, you want to…"

"Kiss you?"

He crossed the room too quickly for her to register his intent and when his hand snaked out and grabbed her arm, surprise rendered her immobile.

She pointedly stared at his hand then coolly met his eyes. "Do not touch me."

"Why not?"

Her heart accelerated as her cheeks became warm. "Because you're being unprofessional."

He gave a mocking snort. "So you can feel it."

"Feel what?"

He slowly ran his palm up, curling long fingers around the soft part of her forearm to gently hold her prisoner. "How it is between us. How it's always been—even when I was off-limits and dating your sister."

She yanked away, severing the moment. "Don't you dare bring that up!"

"It's true."

Yelena took a step back, then another. "But it didn't make it right." She stuck her hands on her hips, guilt and desire now burning her face. "Do you know how many times I wanted to tell Gabriela about us? And every time I psyched myself up to it, she'd bounce in with a stupid grin on her face, telling me how happy she was. I hated myself for lusting after my sister's boyfriend. What we were doing was wrong."

His eyes darkened. "All you and I did was share a few kisses—we did nothing immoral."

"Maybe not in your mind. But every time I was with you—" *I was so damn happy, yet so miserable because* you *made her happy.* "Oh, forget it," she bit off and whirled away, stalking to the door.

Yet just as her hand slapped on the cold wood, she paused. Her feet itched to storm out that door, her fingers falling to clench the polished handle as if it were a lifeline. But the damage was done. She'd not only flung open the gate to their past, she'd blithely charged on through.

With reluctance dogging every second, she turned back. "Alex…about Gabriela."

"What?" He'd grabbed his mobile phone from the desk and was absently checking his messages. "Did she ever manage to sign Jennifer Hawkins to her agency? I knew she was angling for her."

At Yelena's silence he glanced up. "What? She's returning to modeling? She's back in town? She's getting married?" At this last one he gave a snort, part amusement, part skepticism.

"No."

That small word had a truckload of seriousness behind it. His smile faltered, then froze. "What?"

Yelena fingered her necklace and swallowed, the huge lump passing under her skin and down her throat. "Gabriela's dead."

Seconds passed like a yawning chasm, deathly silent yet loaded with meaning.

His entire face tightened into incredulity. "You're kidding."

"Would I lie about something like that? It was never officially announced so there's no way you could've known."

"When?"

"In March. She called me from Spain on Christmas Eve, right after we…you and I…" She trailed off guiltily. Parked in his father's driveway, making out like two teenagers. Half-clothed, his hot mouth on her body, frantic kisses full of hope and promise for the future before she'd breathlessly begged him to stop. *We have to tell Gabriela—she deserves to know.*

"She called me on my way home, desperate for help," Yelena continued. "I tried calling you at the airport but you'd switched your phone off. Then when I landed in Madrid, I kept calling—your mobile, your house. Finally I got some security guy but he wouldn't let me speak to you."

"So you stopped trying."

It wasn't an accusation, just a statement of fact. The truth of it hacked off a little piece of her heart. She *had* just given up.

"I called for a week," she admitted, "but you'd imposed a complete communication blackout. I even told them I was from Bennett & Harper PR, but nothing. I thought you'd…" To her embarrassment, her voice wavered.

Alex's hands went to his hips. "You thought I was breaking up with you?"

"Wouldn't you?" she countered. "I'd left without warning and ended up with Gabriela in a bunch of tiny, off-the-grid towns, some with barely enough sanitation, let alone phone towers. When we finally got to Germany in early March, I found out about your father—a few weeks after you'd been cleared. Then Gabriela's issues, her death, overshadowed everything else."

She held his gaze until he finally glanced away, dragging a hand over his eyes.

"I didn't know. My life has been—" He stopped, dropped his gaze and exhaled forcefully. "I'm sorry about your sister. How did she…?"

"Car crash. She was…" *Impulsive. Reckless. Selfish.* "Gabriela," Yelena finished lamely with a small smile and a shrug.

"And your parents haven't issued a statement?"

"Not through my lack of trying." At his look, her breath caught in her throat, the past and the present mingling to form a heavy mantle of resentment that threatened her composure.

"That's not right, Yelena."

"Yes, well. Gabriela's always been the crazy one—she was the reason we immigrated in the first place. This is just another example of my parents trying to avoid scandalizing the sacred Valero name at any cost."

Her phone went off, intruding on the moment. Quickly she glanced at it. "It's late. I have to go." Ignoring his frown, she pocketed the phone. "I have to feed Bella at six."

She shoved the door open but paused with her hand on the knob. Slowly she turned, fixing him with a steady look. "I'd appreciate you keeping this news to yourself."

At his silent nod she gave him a grateful, fleeting smile. "Thanks. And could you talk with your mother? Let her know why I'm here?"

Again, another nod.

"I'll see you tomorrow."

"Yes."

Then she turned and walked out the door.

Five

Yelena keyed open her suite door and shuffled inside. The cool air hit her face, a wonderful relief against her hot, burning cheeks.

"Jasmine?"

The nanny popped out from the kitchen with a smile, a clean baby bottle in one hand. "Bella's been up for a few minutes. She's a precious little thing, that one."

"She is." She smiled, and the cloying pressure slowly released like a steamer set from boil to off.

"She looks exactly like her mummy, too, all curly dark hair and beautiful skin. I'll bet those gorgeous brown eyes will steal a few hearts."

"I'm counting on it." Yelena grinned as she laid her bag on the glass-topped table. "Before I forget, Jasmine—do you have an invoice for me?"

Jasmine looked confused. "Mr. Rush didn't mention anything about billing you."

Oh. Another revelation in this great, surprise-filled tsunami.

Telling Alex about Gabriela's death had been the right thing to do. And now that guilt no longer weighed on her mind, she could focus more clearly on other things.

Like this campaign.

The pleasant yet confusing hour she'd spent with Pam had only exacerbated her curiosity. Oh, it wasn't anything obvious: Pam was a passionate gardener, encouraging her to smell and touch at every opportunity. But every so often Yelena got that odd, uncomfortable feeling. It wasn't anything Pam said, but rather what she *didn't* say.

It happened every time William Rush's name was mentioned.

For the second time today, a terrible thought surged up but she quickly squashed it down. From one who'd spent years keeping a lid on her emotions, she recognized the same in Pamela Rush. Yet, she acknowledged slowly, some secrets should be kept at all costs.

As the nanny tidied up the last of the dishes, Yelena checked her phone for messages. One from Melanie, wishing her good luck. One from Jonathon, reminding her to check in tomorrow morning. And curiously, one from Carlos—a curt directive to call him back.

He sounded angry.

Yelena placed her phone on the table. She wasn't in the mood for angry, not after the day she'd had.

Pulling the tie from her hair, she ran her fingers through the heavy mass then vigorously rubbed her scalp. She not only had to deal with Alex and all the anxiety his presence entailed, but now there was this strange family tension, something obviously personal that floated below the surface.

Normally she'd question everyone involved, uncover the truth, work out their needs then provide the best possible spin. But something about this situation grated. She'd handled her share of contentious people and their issues but it had never felt quite so personal before.

That ruffled her normally cool composure. Could she be impartial when she still remembered how it felt to have Alex's mouth on hers, his hot breath sending shivers of desire across her skin?

"I'm off." The nanny was at the door, one hand on the knob. "I'll see you tomorrow at seven."

Yelena managed a genuine thank-you but when the door clicked shut, the smile she'd been holding quickly slid away.

With a sigh she padded into the bedroom, her eyes fixed on the crib in the corner. She peered over the edge, holding her breath, but what she saw took the last of it away.

Her baby, her gorgeous girl, blinking sleepily. She'd made a fist and was gently sucking on it with tiny baby grunts, her other hand tightly grasping the rubber end of her brightly colored pacifier.

That's right, bella. *Whatever makes you comfortable in this strange sounding, strange smelling place. You hold on to it.*

She sifted through her work priorities as she changed and fed Bella then settled her back down. As she backed from the room, leaving the door open a bare inch, she glanced back to the living area, to the pile of files on the table, to her iMac ready and waiting to boot up. In the bedroom, she could just hear Bella's tiny settling sounds before she got herself off to sleep.

Her heart wrenched, no less painfully than it had a thousand other times before. Bella, the love of her life, in one room. In the other, her work, the tangible result of her achievements and symbol of her independence. Two opposites, yin and yang tied together to make a whole.

I need a hot shower. The desire was sudden and immediate and she stripped off, leaving the clothes where they fell, then stepped into the enormous bathroom.

She'd checked out the room before, but the opulence of this piece of interior design still took her breath away.

The bathroom dwarfed her bedroom at home, the large sink big enough to bath Bella in. Above, the last rays of the sun streamed in through the huge skylight. The shower on the left boasted plain glass doors, twin showerheads and a half wall of frosted glass bricks.

But it was the spa bath that held her attention. Fashioned like a miniature eternity pool, the blue marble spa ended at the amazing view of Ayers Rock and the red desert soil. One-way, tempered double-glazed glass, she recalled from the brochure in the sitting room.

On the bright-blue marble counter sat a dozen top-end beauty products—creams, lotions, cleansers. Next to it, a golden basket of bath items. With a grin, she selected a green bath bomb and sniffed.

The gorgeous smell of lemongrass and orange sent her toes curling in pleasure and she glanced up to catch her reflection in the large mirror. All these beautiful things, these amazing smells were a temporary distraction. She stared at herself, tilting her head left, then right.

You're twenty-eight. You're successful, you're driven, you're direct. Yet would she have the guts to approach Alex with her concerns about Pam?

It would take timing and subtlety. She'd have to be nonthreatening and put him at ease, something she guessed would be a monumental task.

A flash of apprehension slithered across her face, settling in her dark-brown eyes fringed with long lashes. They were Valero eyes—her father's, Carlos's. And Gabriela's.

The door's tinkling chime shattered the moment and she quickly grabbed a robe before turning from the mirror, leaving the wisps of dread clinging to the ornate bathroom tiles.

Chelsea Rush stood at the door, eyeing the corridor nervously over her shoulder. "Can I come in?"

"Uh...sure."

As Chelsea scuttled past, Yelena gently closed the door. She gave the girl a few moments to fiddle with the decorations, to murmur appreciatively at her iMac then gracefully fall into the huge cream leather sofa.

"I see Alex put you in the Big-Shot Room," the girl finally ventured.

Yelena perched on the sofa arm and smiled. "Really?"

"Yeah. It's our superspecial executive suite for visiting sheikhs, rock stars, prime ministers. I heard one of the Rolling Stones trashed it once and Dad sent him the bill. The bathroom's awesome. And you get freebies."

"So I saw." Yelena moved to the seat. "Must be great living in a place like this."

"Alex and Mum love it."

"And you?"

Chelsea shrugged. "It's better than Canberra. Our house felt like a mausoleum."

The house William Rush died in. "What about school? Your friends?"

She watched the teenager's mouth thin. "I've had tutors since January."

"Ahh." Not exactly a full answer but Yelena let it go. "Can I get you a drink? Soda?"

"No, thank you." Chelsea continued to look around the room, avoiding Yelena's eyes until she lit upon Bella's empty bottle on the dining table. "You have a baby? Here?"

"I do. Her name's Bella."

"Cool. Mum loves babies—she'll probably offer to baby-sit, so watch out." Chelsea grinned. "How old?"

"Five months. She was born on the eighteenth of March."

"I'm a Pisces, too! March fourth. That's funny." She paused then said casually, "Can I ask you a question?"

Despite Chelsea's nonchalance, Yelena knew it wasn't going

to be any ordinary question. Still, she tucked her legs beneath her and sat back, deliberately casual. "Sure."

"Did you mean it about those fashion show tickets?"

Yelena nodded. "Absolutely."

"Why?"

Yelena looked her straight in the eye, smiling. "You remembered my favorite designer. That tells me you're pretty hooked."

"But you don't know me." When Chelsea's brow furrowed, her confusion clear, Yelena swallowed. What could she say that wouldn't break Alex's request for confidentiality? "I mean…you're Gabriela's sister and all—"

"Exactly." Yelena thankfully grasped the straw. "And I know what it's like when no one else gets what you love. It'll be a fun way to get to know each other. Believe it or not, it's been a while since I got out." At the teenager's continued silence, Yelena said softly, "But if you think your mum won't approve…"

"No, it's not that," Chelsea said, her gaze skittering away. "I just… well… Alex told me and Mum he's hired you to handle the press. So why would you want to…why are you—?" She scowled, as if annoyed by her lack of eloquence.

Yelena almost sighed in relief. "Why am I offering to socialize on private time?"

"Yeah. All that stuff they're printing about my dad. About him cheating on Mum—"

"Chelsea. You can't take any notice of that. The press make stuff up all the time. I'm here to help take the focus off that."

"But that's the thing…" When she lifted her chin, the tortured look in those shimmering blue pools stunned Yelena. "I think it *is* true."

Six

The firm knock on the door made them both jump. For a second they both sat there, staring at each other, until Yelena finally found her voice.

"Who is it?"

"Alex."

Chelsea leapt to her feet, shaking her head.

"Just a minute," Yelena called then turned to the panicky girl.

"We had a row... I'm supposed to be in my room... I have to go!"

"Chelsea—"

"Shh!" Chelsea hurried over to the patio doors and swept them open. Cold night air swirled in. "I can get back through the lagoon walk. I'll talk to you later."

And then she was gone.

Mind racing, Yelena slowly closed the glass doors, crossed the living room and opened the door.

Alex stood there in his shirt-sleeves, tie and top buttons askew.

She pulled the robe tight around her waist as her stomach gave a weird little flip. "I was just about to have a shower."

"Okay."

He remained there, silent, until she said slowly, "Did you need me for something?"

A minuscule smile pulled the corner of his mouth for a second before it disappeared. "We need to talk about a few things."

Could she handle any more today? With an inward sigh, Yelena pulled the door wider. "If you want to wait, you can come in."

"Sure."

Alex was not a patient man. While she was in the shower he sat on the couch for all of twenty seconds. He knew because he counted every single one. When he realized what he was doing, he shot to his feet and grabbed the remote, flicking on the huge plasma television. Pretty soon he clicked that off and started to pace but eventually ended up staring out at the night lights through the window. Another five minutes and his patience felt as if it had been put through a shredder. Twice.

Normally, once he'd dismissed something from his mind, it stayed gone. Yet his second thoughts about Yelena's involvement in Carlos's scheme had bizarrely festered, chewing away at his thoughts until he realized he had to take action. It had only increased in urgency after his one-sided conversation with Chelsea thirty minutes before.

Yet as the minutes ticked by his thoughts were not on his sister's sullen countenance but on Yelena. Yelena in the shower. Naked. Hot water running over her silky skin, making it slick and slippery—

"What did you want to talk about?"

He whirled, swallowing a groan. She stood in the entry

wrapped in a Diamond Bay robe, her long hair tousled and damp, curling down her back.

The urgent craving to kiss her—hard—engulfed him.

Almost as if he'd voiced the desire, she rocked onto her back foot. "Alex? Has something happened?"

His groin tightened as he bit off a bitter laugh. *Yeah, something's happened.* With a deep breath, he forced his mouth into a smile.

"I ordered room service."

She blinked then grabbed her clothes where she'd tossed them on the floor. "Thank you. But that wasn't necessary."

"I thought we could discuss this campaign over dinner." When she paused in her folding he smiled again, this time a sincere one. "You have to eat."

The silence stood for a few seconds until she nodded. "I'll get dressed."

Yelena whirled on her heel, forcing herself not to run into the bedroom and slam the door. *It's business. Remember that.* Yet everything she remembered of Alex contradicted that hollow statement.

After vigorously rubbing her still-damp hair, she quickly stepped into underwear then shoved on a pair of soft pink cashmere track pants and a plain black T-shirt, securing her hair into a high ponytail. A quick check of Bella deep in sleep and she was ready to face Alex. One deep, fortifying breath—okay, two—and she finally walked out into the lounge room.

The sight of him made that last breath shudder in her chest. Even with his back to her, he still commanded her focus. Tall and muscular, that was Alex. He always made her feel feminine, even delicate, which was no mean feat given her height. His wide shoulders were capable of taking on a hundred worries, weathering any crisis. He was like a house built on iron-clad foundations.

She'd once overheard Carlos describe him as "entitled and

arrogant" but she knew all too well strength and conviction could be misinterpreted as arrogance by some.

As he shifted, her eyes went to the curve of his neck, to the tanned exposed skin just above his collar.

Her body tightened as a bolt of desire shot through every womanly part. She knew how he felt beneath those clothes, that solid chest, those sweetly curved biceps, the delicious way his muscles bunched and rippled beneath hot, touchable skin.

As her senses prickled with remembrance, she watched Alex shuffle through the press clippings she'd left open on the table. It took a few moments to recognize his expression but when she did it sent her back a step.

Every muscle in his face, every line had contracted into something so blatantly raw and painful that it made her throat constrict. This whole situation affected him more than he'd ever admit. As she watched him flick through the clippings, a soft curse crossed his lips.

Her heart ached for him at that moment, compassion propelling her forward.

"It's a weird paradox, isn't it?" she said softly.

He turned, the shutters descending as he placed a hand on the stack. "What? Being eviscerated by the press?"

"Having people think you've gotten away with murder, yet being hounded by every news outlet for your exclusive story."

"You get used to it."

"No, you don't." She went to the table and shuffled the clippings back into their folder, determinedly ignoring the minuscule distance separating them. Yet she couldn't ignore the way her entire body tingled under his scrutiny. "No one could."

"And you know what it's been like for me."

She snapped her chin up, barely catching the tail end of his look—a mixture of derision and irritation.

Something inside her gave way. "I've been there, Alex. It may have been on a small scale, I may have only been fifteen but I remember every single humiliating detail." She shoved her hands on her hips, back rigid. "It's all the Spanish press covered for weeks—'Gabriela, the wild twelve-year-old druggie daughter of Senator Juan Valero.' They'd follow us to school, bribe our friends for an exclusive. One even broke into our summer house. We couldn't function, couldn't *breathe* without causing a headline. We moved to Australia to get away from that." She paused for a breath, her face hot. "So don't tell me I don't know what it's like. I've lived it."

Alex stared at her, at the tightly controlled, elegant fury beneath that icy demeanor.

She frowned. "Gabriela never told you?"

"No. She just said your father was appointed to the Spanish embassy."

"He chased that appointment, much to my mother's horror. In her opinion, Australia was an uncultured backwater. My father spent a lot of time and money—not to mention kissing up—to ensure our past faded away."

"So that's why…" At her raised eyebrow, he finished off with, "You're a peacemaker. You always have been."

She shrugged, dropping her eyes. "Am I?"

"Yes. I've never seen you deliberately start an argument."

"Oh, I've started a few," she said dryly.

"Not in public. And I reckon that's why you're in PR. It's why you're so good at it. You know, creating calm in the face of public frenzy."

She blinked, faintly chagrined. "Maybe."

"Definitely." It didn't take a genius to figure that out. Before now he'd never fully recognized Yelena's obsession for calming waves. Yet it was hardly surprising, given what she'd been through. And, he realized, if one person could drag the Rush name out of the gutter, someone who was passionate, compelled and committed, it was Yelena.

Something must have given him away, something he'd let slip that showed on his face, because she was smiling at him, her first honest-to-goodness smile since she'd walked into her office at Bennett & Harper.

"Alex, I need to ask you about—"

"Mmm?"

Yelena swallowed as a familiar look passed over his features. It was his frankly provocative "I want to taste you" look—*that look*—that made her blood zing, exciting all her womanly bits, making her wish for one insane second that he'd do exactly what his eyes promised and kiss her.

The fight-or-flight response snaked low in her gut, her brain commanding her to run. Her leg muscles tingled in preparation, waiting for the signal.

Then the doorbell chimed and she nearly jumped a foot in the air. A fact Alex didn't miss, judging by his grin. She shot him a glare and went to answer the door, unsure if relief or annoyance tossed in her stomach. Both felt dissatisfying.

The waiter swept in and began to set up the meal. By the time he'd left, it was as if their little exchange had never happened. Which was fine considering she'd other things to focus on right now: her stomach began to rumble as Alex removed the warming lids with a flourish.

He'd ordered a large platter of assorted seafood—barbequed calamari, beer-batter fish and delicately crumbed scallops. To one side, there was a bowl of fresh salad with three separate dressings. Next to that, a bowl of crisp chips accompanied by a dish of dressing and crumbly sea salt.

He watched her closely. "You approve?"

"You know I do." Seafood and chips were her favorite—he knew that. A reluctant smile tugged at her mouth. A peace offering?

Then he was pulling out her chair. "Shall we eat?"

Despite Alex's declaration that they needed to discuss business, they filled their plates in silence, two people resolutely focused on that small act of polite domesticity. Yet after Yelena had taken a bite of her food her taste buds exploded, clearing her brain of all else.

"This is amazing!" She savored the delicate flavor of calamari.

Alex smiled, chewing away. "All credit goes to Franco. I stole him from Icebergs in Sydney. Try the chips with the aioli."

She speared a chunky golden chip with her fork, obediently dipping it into the creamy white dressing.

Luxury burst over her tongue and she gave another appreciative groan. But what did her in was Alex's sensual mouth, curved up in amusement. It brought back a moment of pure unadulterated desire so powerful that it staggered her.

"Told you," he murmured before shoving another forkful in his mouth, chewing slowly without taking his eyes from her.

That all-knowing gaze recorded her every movement, from the faltering breath she drew, to the gradual exhale. It was keenly familiar, that almost promissory glint in his eyes, as if the past few months had ceased to exist and he was once again all hers.

Her skin felt so warm she was sure her temperature had risen a few degrees, the air so thick she had trouble clearing her throat. But finally she did.

"I've had a few ideas for your campaign."

A brief flicker of surprise shadowed his eyes. "That was quick."

"That's what you hired me for."

She'd deliberately steered their conversation into neutral waters. So what prompted her tiny pang of disappointment when his eyes suddenly turned serious?

"Go on."

"I think we should start with something local. Some kind of party or celebration that includes the community and Diamond Bay employees." She placed her cutlery on the table and leaned forward. "This resort employs thousands and generates some major tourist dollars. Your tenth anniversary is next year, right?" At his nod, she continued. "So as a lead-up, you could host a party—say the first of September for the first day of spring. It could be a showcase for local talent, too. Chefs, musicians. Artists. Decorators. We can have a main marquee for the art and decorations, then a separate one for the music. And outside we can set up long tables for the food, with Diamond Bay covering any shortfall. It'd be a social and practical event rolled into one."

She paused for a breath, looking at Alex expectantly. But when he remained silent, her broad smile faltered. "Well? What do you think?"

"The first is two weeks away," he finally said.

"I've organized other events in less time. And because we'd be using a lot of external resources and labor, Diamond Falls' workload will be less."

"I see."

"We'd need one of your legal people to take care of the insurance. We'd also need a supplier liaison and a press person. I checked your staff directory—you have a dedicated press office and a banquets division, yes?"

"Yes." He gave his attention to his plate, where he proceeded to cut into a piece of fish with one clean slice. "You've given this some thought."

"I have. Actually, the idea came from your mother."

He looked up, capturing her eyes as he slowly placed the food in his mouth. Yelena nodded. "She was talking about the local talent—musicians, artists—and how she wanted to get involved with them, promote their work to a wider audience."

"I see," was all he said as he chewed. *How could he not*

know this? Finally swallowing, he added, "Do you have some figures, details?"

"I'll need to speak with one of your accounts people… tomorrow?"

He reached for his wineglass and cradled it gently in his hand. "I'll arrange it."

"Great!" Yelena felt relief shade the edges of her satisfied smile and with a nod she refocused on her meal.

Thankfully, discussing local businesses and the physical logistics of arranging the event kept them talking until after coffee. But when Alex called room service to clear the table, Yelena's good mood shattered with her ringing phone.

It was Carlos.

"Where are you?"

"Why?" With a glance at Alex, she quickly walked down the hall and into the bathroom.

"Are you with—" he paused, then almost spat out the words "—Alex Rush?"

"Again, why?" She gently closed the door.

"Dammit, Yelena! I told you to stay away from him."

"You've told me nothing of the sort."

"I would've thought my silence on the subject didn't need elaboration."

She glared at her reflection in the mirror. "I'm not a mind reader, Carlos."

His huff of impatience cranked up her irritation. "What's gotten into you? You used to be so…"

"Compliant?"

"Sensible. People have been talking."

Something in his tone bothered her. A lot. "So what's new?" At his aggrieved sigh, she narrowed her eyes and leaned back on the door. "What? Can't I go about my daily business without some gossip spreading lies?"

Carlos was quick to latch on to that. "So he's a client?"

"I didn't say that."

"But that's what you meant." He sighed. "You need to get yourself a boyfriend, Yelena."

His sanctimoniousness rankled, tiny pinpricks stinging her skin. "Maybe *he's* my boyfriend, Carlos. Maybe he's decided to set me up as his bought-and-paid-for mistress and I'm going to dance naked for him every night. Whatever the reason, it's none of your damn business!"

She jammed her finger on the disconnect button, cloying heat choking her throat. But as she yanked the bathroom door open, she nearly ran smack-bang into Alex.

At the last second she sprang back, skillfully avoiding his steadying hands.

"Everything okay?"

"Fine." She gave him a belligerent look, straightened her T-shirt over her hips and tossed her head.

"Doesn't sound like it."

"It's Carlos." She brushed past him, too irritated to acknowledge the little zing as his body heat briefly enveloped her. "He's being an ass."

Yet as angry as she was, she could still feel Alex's presence close behind as they returned to the living room. "He's…" She threw her hands in the air before flopping down onto the sofa.

"Being Carlos?"

"Yeah."

When she fixed him with a considering look, he met it steadily.

"He thinks you and I…we…" She broke off, feeling the warmth on her cheeks. "I have no idea how he knew I was here."

The tiny stab of guilt hit Alex low. Of course he'd made sure Carlos knew. "Does it matter?"

"It does to him. What on earth did you do to him?"

His jaw tightened involuntarily. Yet his calm words belied

the fury simmering under the surface. "Maybe it's not all my fault."

"I didn't say it was." She frowned, glancing away. "But it's odd. Why would he think we're involved? He's never seen us together...I mean," she added with a flush, "*romantically*. Has he?"

"Not that I know of."

She went on, almost absently, "Sure, we've been to parties, official functions, but we've never been alone—"

"Except at the Christmas ball in July. In the kitchen."

The flush on her face remained, his slow smile aiding its presence. "And I've never been to your office or—" She broke off, eyes rounding. "I have. Once. And Carlos was there."

"When?"

She frowned. "It was September the first. Gabriela's birthday. I remember because she was running late and asked me to pick up the cake then double-check you'd left already. Your..." She paused, swallowing. "Your father turned up."

They both stared at each other. Alex needed no further reminder of that night: it was seared like a permanent scar on his heart. And like the flick of a switch, that hostile, fury-ridden confrontation came screaming back.

You've got a warped sense of what marriage means. Stay the hell away from her or by God I will—

You'll do what? William Rush had spat back. *This is my family*—mine! *No one's lacked for anything. No one would be anything if it weren't for me!*

And you've been destroying us for years, you selfish bastard!

He shook his head, refusing to let the black wave drag him down into that hellhole again. "Carlos was there?"

Yelena nodded slowly. "I saw him leave as I was getting the cake from the kitchen. After we—" her body prickled as she finished lamely "—were in your office."

Alex stared at her in silence, his mind ticking like an overheated engine.

If Carlos had been there…if he'd heard… Then this meant—

He was so sure he'd been right, so hell-bent on bundling the Valeros into one tainted basket that he'd failed to allow for one major flaw.

That Yelena hadn't blabbed to Carlos after all.

He sprang to his feet, realization sending licking flames of humility through his gut. "I have to go."

"Alex?"

He ignored her confused question. Instead he strode across the room, jerked the door open then walked out, refusing to look back.

Seven

Tuesday flew by in a flurry of meetings, phone calls and budget preparations. After liaising with Alex's press and banquet staff, she spent the night working late at the dining table in her suite, organizing, planning, checking then rechecking. The Rushes were first and foremost in her mind, from Alex's odd departure last night to her continued concern about Pam. As for Chelsea… When she'd dropped in with lunch, it was as if her cryptic admission had been erased from history. Instead, they chatted about movies, books and fashion, until work called and Yelena was again swamped.

On Wednesday morning as she booted up her laptop in her temporary office, her mobile phone rang.

It was Juan Valero.

"Hola, Papá."

"Yelena, Carlos told us about your new client."

"Told you what?" Yelena replied in Spanish, shoving her phone under her chin while reaching for a folder on the long desk.

The pause was significant enough for her to frown. Then her father said firmly, "It's Alexander Rush."

"And how would Carlos know?"

"Is it true?"

Yelena sighed and swiveled back to her laptop. She could never lie to her father. "Yes, but it's confidential. You can't say anything to anyone."

"I do not gossip, Yelena." She swallowed nervously. His stern rebuke made her feel nine years old all over again. "And is getting mixed up with that family a wise move?"

His condescending tone irked her. "It's my job, *Papá*."

She could feel the waves of displeasure thunder down the phone. "You are a Valero."

And you remind me every chance you get. "And..?"

"I do not appreciate your tone, Yelena," Juan snapped. "The man has been accused of murder."

"He was not charged."

"Nonetheless, it is not the sort of person—or family—I wish you to associate with."

Uncharacteristic rebellion bubbled up. "My boss decides my clients, not me."

"And what happens when you make partner? Will you get to decide then?"

She glanced up to see Chelsea at the door with a tentative smile, holding a tray. "Can we talk about this later? I have to go."

"Yelena—"

"*Papá*, I'm working."

His aggrieved sigh came down the line. "We will talk when you return home." And he hung up.

Yelena slowly placed her phone back on the desk.

"Breakfast?" Chelsea asked casually and slid the tray onto the conference table. "I didn't see you this morning and I checked—you didn't order room service." She quickly glanced around. "You know, this room *is* a bit spare. Needs more color."

Yelena tipped her head, considering. From Chelsea's overly nonchalant stance to the way her eyes darted, the teenager had more than interior decorating on her mind. "Something blue would be nice."

"And a comfy sofa, a few pillows…" Chelsea trailed off, arranging the cutlery before lifting the warming trays. "There's toast, coffee and fruit. If you don't like, I can always get Franco to make something more fancy…."

"When it comes to food, I'm not a 'fancy' kind of girl." Yelena smiled. "Toast and fruit is great."

They both tackled the food, munching contentedly in silence. After her second piece of toast, Yelena placed her cup of coffee on the table.

"Chelsea. Can we talk about what you said the other night? About your father?"

Chelsea flicked a quick glance at the closed door, her eyes running across the long glass wall to the offices beyond. Her chin went up a fraction. "What about it?"

Such bravado for one so young. Yelena warmed her hands on the cup and leaned forward with a smile. "You know, Gabriela told me you were friends. She used to call you 'Chelsea-bun.'"

Chelsea grinned. "Yeah."

"Between you and me, I think she liked you better than Alex." Yelena winked.

Chelsea laughed then, a sudden rusty sound that made Yelena think she didn't do enough of it.

Then suddenly her smile froze. "What do you mean, 'liked'?"

Yelena looked the confused girl straight in the eye. "I'm going to trust you with something. I've been asked not to announce it, but I think you should know. I'm sorry, Chelsea, but there's no way to put this gently. Gabriela...well, she died."

As Chelsea gaped, mouth wide open, Yelena leaned forward and took her hand.

"How? When...?" She finally managed to choke out, her eyes filling.

"In March. We were in Germany and she was taken to hospital. She'd lost a lot of blood and they just couldn't save her...." Yelena ducked her head as the wave of grief pulled at her legs, threatening to tug her under.

"So it was an accident? Car?"

Faced with the teenager's pooling tears, Yelena could only nod. *Forgive me for the little white lie,* she offered up. *But you know it's necessary.*

With a wrenching sob, Chelsea was suddenly in her arms. Together they held each other, Yelena holding back tears for the death of a sister she'd been forbidden to acknowledge, Chelsea crying for the loss of a friend.

Eventually Chelsea pulled away, swiping at her cheeks self-consciously. Yelena handed her a tissue and offered a smile. "I'm sorry for not telling you sooner."

"That's okay." Chelsea sat back down, her hands shoved between her knees as she leaned forward in her seat.

Yelena began to stack their plates, giving Chelsea time to compose herself.

"I miss her," Chelsea said suddenly.

Yelena nodded. "Yeah, I do, too."

"She... she was the only one I told stuff to."

Yelena paused, giving the girl her full attention. "Like what?"

"Stuff." Chelsea shrugged, her eyes going to Yelena's neat plate stack. She reached for her glass and stuck the straw in her mouth. "What I wanted to do with my life, the places I wanted to visit. She'd been to so many countries and had heaps of stories."

Yelena smiled. "She loved to travel. She used to brag she'd seen every country except Alaska and the Poles."

"Yeah." Chelsea returned the smile. "She was gorgeous but not in a bitchy way, you know? She always had time for me." She tipped her head, studying Yelena. "Like you."

Something warm and satisfying spread across Yelena's heart. "Thank you."

When Chelsea stiffened and glanced up, Yelena followed her eyes to the shadow beyond the glass wall. A second later Alex swung the door open with firm intent.

"It's nine-thirty," he said, glancing from one to the other from his position in the doorway.

"Sure is," Yelena answered, downing the last of her coffee before placing the cup on the tray.

"You've eaten?"

Yelena nodded to their empty plates. "Yep."

"Good."

Alex remained fixed to the spot, hands jammed in his pockets, his casual silence in direct contrast to the tension radiating from his stance. Yelena frowned.

"Did you need something?" she finally ventured.

Alex turned to Chelsea who was slurping her juice with purposeful intent. "Don't you have a class to go to?"

"Not yet."

A ghost of a frown creased his forehead. "Where's Mum?"

"Watching TV."

"What?"

"I dunno, something." Chelsea waved her hand.

"Why don't you go and see if she wants breakfast?"

"I think she's already—"

"Chelsea. Go."

"Fine." In a huff she grabbed up her bag, paused then with a pointed look at her brother, noisily slurped down the last of her juice.

"Go!"

"I'm going!" With a smile and nod at Yelena, Chelsea bounced from the room.

Yelena's mouth tweaked, only to waver when Alex gently closed the door behind him.

"How is your…" He paused then added, "Bella?"

"She's fine."

"Does she need anything?"

Yelena smiled. "Apart from food, sleep, a nappy change and brief entertainment? No. She's only five months old."

"Right."

Yelena tipped her head to the side. "You were what, fifteen when Chelsea was born?"

He nodded. "But I didn't see a lot of her. She was mostly with nannies and housekeepers."

"Your mum seems more like a 'get her hands dirty' kind of parent," Yelena ventured.

"Dad's idea. He was courting investors at the time and needed a wife on his arm."

"Oh." Another unfavorable mark against William Rush. Yelena couldn't imagine not being there for the feeding, the bathing, all the little changes and milestones that made parenthood a constant, wondrous delight.

Her thoughts must have given her away because Alex's brow raised in a slow question.

"Oh, nothing…"

"Tell me," Alex said, leaning against the edge of her desk.

"It's just…" She reached out to shuffle some papers into a neat pile, avoiding his eyes. "I know a lot of people who've gone from school, then uni, to some you-beaut job, focusing on climbing the corporate ladder. They work hard, they party harder, but they're still waiting for something to give their life meaning. A grand passion." She remained intent on rearranging her desk, this time slotting pens into a cup. "A baby is a life-changing experience. It opened up my heart in a new way." She finally glanced up, almost apologetically, as a faint flush spread across her cheeks. "But then, I imagine all mothers feel that way."

A thin film of self-disgust coated Alex's tongue. Quickly he swallowed it. What kind of jerk was he to make her feel embarrassed about that? "The good ones, at least."

She gave him a tiny smile then seemed to gather herself together. "So…do you want to see what I've been working on?"

With a firm nod, Alex pulled up a chair and sat. Thankfully she hadn't mentioned his abrupt departure Monday night and frankly, he'd spent ages trying to wrap his head around it all.

He'd been so damn sure of her involvement that he'd not stopped to think of the possibility of this mess just being Carlos's doing. That Yelena could actually be blameless hadn't factored in at all. So he'd spent yesterday getting things straight in his head, until he'd clicked online and read the late-edition papers.

A painful mix of fury and disgust had tightened his stomach. Another page of salacious lies about William Rush blinked onto his screen, this time from an "anonymous lover."

He'd felt like chucking the monitor across the room. Instead he'd downed one shot of top-notch bourbon, the burning alcohol a painful reminder why he never drank the stuff, before hurling the glass onto the patio where it shattered with a satisfying smash. Yet as he picked up the pieces, his thoughts turned not to Carlos, but to Yelena.

Christ, when had a decision—any decision—been this bloody difficult?

With Yelena now here, his plans half-complete, he realized he still needed her. As his PR person, yes, because she was damn good at what she did. And Pam and Chelsea seemed to like her. But now, as he gave her his full attention, a different kind of need began to filter in as the minutes ticked by. If it wasn't her "come here and smell me" scent twisting his insides, then it was the way she lit up as she got into her spiel. She gestured in typical European fashion, using her whole body to convey her message. When she smiled, her mouth made tiny dimples in her cheeks.

In the past he'd tried to make her smile as much as possible.

So the blame for the press leaks lay firmly at Carlos's feet. But she still had a child, one that wasn't his.

Did it twist his gut every time he thought about Yelena and some faceless guy in bed together? Hell, yes.

Why?

Because...because... He tightened his jaw and stared at the figures Yelena slid across the desk.

She's mine.

Fierce possessiveness snaked through his body, sending it into a craving, bittersweet ache. He still wanted her in his bed—that much hadn't changed.

"As you can see, the costs for decorations will be—" She ended up on a gasp as he reached for the papers and got her hand instead.

Their gazes collided and held. Her eyes rounded before those long lashes fluttered down, severing the moment when she withdrew.

For a perverse second, he craved something more. But then it was gone and amazingly, the loss saddened him.

After a moment's study of the papers, he said, "So let's hear the rest of your plan."

With a nervous swallow, Yelena began. "So after the party, your mother suggested focusing on the local community."

At his curious look, she continued, "She's got a deep love of this area and really wants to help the people, like setting up a scholarship program and donating to a few charities."

"And what about her work in Canberra? Won't that suffer if she's taking on more?"

"Alex…" She hesitated. "Did she not tell you?"

"Tell me what?"

With a flush, she said, "I thought Pam told you. Yesterday we talked and she—"

"Tell me what?"

Yelena frowned. "She's still officially donating to those charities. But she resigned from the boards."

His mouth flattened into a grim line. "I see."

"Pam *wanted* to resign. Alex, listen to me. She hated the politics and after those rumors started spreading, she—" She paused then said, "Look, I don't want to get in the middle of family issues here—"

"You're not. I told them both why you're here, which should make your job a lot easier."

Yelena knew this wasn't about the campaign. But she still nodded. "Thank you. But if we're all not on the same page—"

"I'm doing this for them," he said tightly.

"I know. But they may have differing opinions. Chelsea, for one, seems—" she paused, searching for the right word "—hostile. Why don't I organize a meeting so we can talk things over?"

At his inscrutable countenance, Yelena's heart crumbled a little. "I'm here to help you. All of you," she continued.

He pointed at the paper, shrugging off her concern. "And this?"

Yelena sighed then picked one page up. "A list of press we'll be alerting for the party, which will start around four p.m. and go on after sunset. We also need to work on the guest list. Pam's given me hers, so it's just up to you."

He barely glanced at the list before his eyes came back to her. "Have dinner with me."

She blinked, confused. "Sorry?"

"Have dinner with me."

"Why?"

"Why not?"

She leaned back in her chair. "I don't work after six."

"A baby sleeps, Yelena. A lot."

Yelena stared at him while he maintained composure with ridiculous ease. Her mind quickly flicked through the pros and cons of his invitation. The little morsels of information he'd shared about his family weren't enough. There were still too many questions. Surely she could spend one evening eating dinner to uncover more?

"Okay."

The half smile he gave her curled her toes and like Pavlov's dog, she smiled blindly back, heart racing.

"Excellent." He rose, taking her notes with him. "Wear jeans and be in the lobby at six-twenty."

"Wait—I thought we were eating in my room?"

That smile again, this time with a slightly decadent edge. "The fresh air will do you good. I'll organize Jasmine for Bella. Six-twenty."

When he was gone, Yelena realized too late that a smiling, charming Alexander Rush was way more worrisome than an angry, combative one.

Eight

Later that day, Yelena was in her suite working on her laptop while Chelsea sat cross-legged on her lounge room carpet.

"How long have you been dating my brother?"

Absently, Yelena looked up from her laptop. "What makes you think we're dating?"

"Oh, come on!" Chelsea rolled her eyes in mock derision and recrossed her legs. "You've both got that look about you— that 'I want to jump on you as soon as we're alone' vibe."

"Chelsea!" What the devil could she say without outright lying? But damn, the girl was intuitive, she had to give her that. "That's… that's…"

"None of my business?" Chelsea picked up a rattle and gently waved it in front of a gurgling Bella.

"Exactly." She managed to hide her grin behind her laptop. Then she closed it with a sigh and stood, giving her back a good stretch. "Now I have to go and have a shower."

"For dinner, huh?"

"Well, yeah."

"With Aaaaalex?" Chelsea winked, making kissy sounds.

"You…!"

Chelsea squealed and ducked as a small sofa pillow flew harmlessly past.

With a wide smile Yelena scooped up Bella and marched off down the hall. But when she emerged half an hour later, all primed and polished, the look Chelsea gave was frankly disapproving.

"What?" Yelena did a three-sixty, tweaking the drop-shoulder of her purple knitted sweater.

"What's with that tight hairdo?"

Yelena's hand went up to the French roll she'd painstakingly secured. "You don't like it?"

"No. Let your hair fall down but have the sides up. Go to the mirror and I'll show you."

The teenager sat her on a dining chair in front of the hallway mirror then flicked on the light.

"You're good at this," Yelena said as Chelsea began to deftly refix her long curls. "Ever thought of a career in fashion?"

"All the time."

"So why don't you?" Yelena asked.

She caught the glimmer in Chelsea's eyes just before she refocused on Yelena's hair. "Because it's complicated. Alex and I had a row the other night. I *am* good at tennis and a lot of money's gone into my training. And Alex and Mum—"

"Forget about what other people think for one second. What do *you* want to do?"

"I want…" Her voice drifted off then she added firmly, "To study fashion design. Maybe work at a magazine. There. You're done."

Yelena stood. "Then you should do that."

As they both stared at Yelena's reflection, Yelena could feel the mood take on a subtle change. And when she met

Chelsea's eyes through the mirror, she saw something flash across the girl's face.

"I need to tell you something...something personal."

"Okay." Yelena turned, giving the teen her full attention.

"It was my father... I..." Chelsea's eyes skittered away before coming back in sudden defiance. "I want to make a statement. A public statement. Can you help me write a press release?"

Yelena's brow furrowed. "About what?"

"I'm sick and tired of everyone making out like my father was some kind of living god."

The sudden venom in Chelsea's voice forced Yelena back a step. After a moment, she said slowly, "What did he do, Chelsea?"

Chelsea glanced to the door. When she spoke, it all tumbled out in a tight whisper. "He was a control freak. I mean, *major*. All of my friends were handpicked because of their parents. I played tennis because it was fun but then *he* decided I needed a coach and then it was four hours a day, every day. It sucked. He went mental when I said I wanted to do designing. And..." She petered off and glanced away. "He treated Mum like an idiot, always checking what she wore, who she saw. He'd start yelling over some stupid little thing, and she'd... I'd..." She flushed and glanced away, fiddling with the hem of her frayed T-shirt. "It'll take more than a few nasty articles to do him justice."

"Chelsea..." As the pieces in Yelena's head began to slowly click into place, a horrible thought occurred. "Do you have proof about his cheating?"

Here she looked uncomfortable. "No. But I wouldn't be surprised if he was."

"Have you talked to Alex about this?"

"No." She shook her head. "This is my problem. I didn't want to lump this on his plate, not with everything else that's been going on."

Yelena's mind began to toss. "I think—"

The bell to the front door chimed.

"That'll be Jasmine. Look, Chelsea," she said softly, placing her hands on the girl's shoulders. "I'd strongly suggest you talk to your mother about this first. Let her know how you feel and see if you can both come up with something together. Then we can talk it over with Alex, okay?"

Chelsea's blue eyes churned with all the intensity of a storm at sea. "Okay."

"Good. I want to help you."

Chelsea nodded then jerked her head to the door. "You'd better go. Alex is a bear when he's left waiting."

Yelena rolled her eyes and gave her a smile. "I know."

As Yelena stepped out from the swooshing glass entrance doors, the sight of Alex stopped her heart for a second.

Oh, mercy me. He was every woman's bad-boy fantasy in hard-core black leather—from the jacket that stretched across broad shoulders, down to tight pants that cupped a perfect behind and high-topped boots encasing long legs.

She grabbed her necklace and ran her thumb over the smooth glass. Pounding blood sped to her head, sending her skin into a full body flush. And when he glanced up from checking his watch and spotted her, the will-melting smile he gave made her want to run right into his arms and kiss him.

That just would not do.

Flustered, she glanced around, her eyes coming to rest on a shiny, sleek...

"Motorbike."

Alex's smile broadened and her breath hooked again. "Not just any motorbike... A Shinya Kimura. The man's a legend when it comes to customizing." He slowly ran his hand over the mirrored metal, taking his time to savor the polished surface.

Yelena swallowed, suppressing a small shiver at his unguarded raw joy.

"And it's the only way to see the Outback. Here." He tossed her a helmet from the seat then grabbed his.

Obediently she pulled it over her head then fiddled with the clip.

"Let me." With his warm fingers at her jaw she tried not to think about how eagerly her body reacted to him, how she secretly thrilled at the slightest contact.

While she stood there like a nervous teenager on a first date, he reached across the seat and produced a leather jacket. Slowly, with the deft intimacy of a familiar lover, he spread the jacket around her shoulders, waiting until she'd got it on before zipping it up.

In the cold, still night, she heard every single suggestive snick of those metal teeth snapping together, a signal for her blood to pump in earnest while she tried to control her runaway thoughts.

He slowly dragged the zipper up, the bright blue depths of his eyes sparking with humor... and something much more dangerous. Her hand jerked reflexively, seeking the comfort of her necklace before she realized what she was doing and forced it back down. His keen eyes didn't miss that, judging by the way his mouth tweaked into a smile.

Then suddenly he withdrew. "All done. Let's go."

Desperate to focus on something else, she stared at the bike and drew a slow, steady breath into her lungs.

"How do I get on?"

He grinned, threw a leg over the bike then glanced expectantly over his shoulder. "Like that."

Okay. With a nod she placed her hands on his shoulders, centered her weight then threw her leg over.

Thanks to the seat angle, she immediately slid forward and her crotch bumped firmly against his butt. She quickly wiggled back but Alex slapped her lightly on the thigh.

"Stop moving. You'll upset the balance."

He swiftly kick-started the engine and the bike leapt to life in one almighty roar.

"Hold on!" Alex yelled over the noise as the bike jumped forward with a gutsy growl. Yelena squealed, grabbed Alex's waist and they slowly made their way out onto the single road leading from Diamond Bay.

It was a strange and wonderful experience, her first time on a motorbike. The speed, the air streaming over her body, the absolute vulnerability of being out in the open, forced a laugh from her throat. As they flew along the road, she was swept up by exhilaration, her lips stretching in a wide smile. It was natural, automatic that she settle farther into the seat, wedging herself firmly up against Alex's wide back, his powerful leather-clad muscles in total control of the throbbing beast beneath them.

Yet as the minutes stretched and the road got more rugged as they sped towards Ayers Rock, one thing was becoming increasingly obvious. She was getting turned on.

At first she thought it was the throbbing metal beneath her butt, or maybe the way Alex's legs felt between her thighs, the heat from those hard muscles seeping through her jeans. It certainly didn't help that there were only thin layers of worn denim between her body and his. No, all those things did affect her, but it was every tiny bump in the tarmac that sent reverberating vibrations through her skin, stimulating her senses into overdrive.

After the second little surprise, she gave an inward groan and bit down on her lip. *Damn.* With her crotch wedged snugly up against Alex's backside, raw sensation shot up her body, arousal tingling at every tiny jolt.

By the time Alex slowed down, her mouth felt as if she'd indulged in a slightly rough, hour-long kissing session.

When they finally stopped, Yelena's legs wobbled as he helped her from the bike.

"It's a bit rough at first—you'll get used to it." He pulled off his helmet, a smile crinkling his eyes into wicked humor which only exacerbated her predicament further.

Get used to it? Did that mean he was planning on staying in her life? She removed her helmet and shook her hair out just before Alex grabbed her shoulders and pivoted her.

"What—?"

"Check that out."

With the setting sun at their backs, the sky had taken on a dusky blue-grey tinge, a smattering of cloud spreading across the sky like thin cobwebs. And smack-bang in the middle sat Ayers Rock, its burnt orange body seeming to swell and glow as the sun crept farther down.

Seconds edged into minutes as they both stood there, watching the sky deepen and darken, changing the Rock's orange into fiery red then eventually burnt amber.

Speechless, Yelena watched the light stretch farther and farther until finally, Ayers Rock became one massive, dark shadow on the horizon.

"Wow," she finally breathed.

"Yep. As stunning and unique as Diamond Falls is, I never get sick of seeing that." He put a hand at her back. "Shall we eat?"

He guided her towards glowing lights and they emerged from the scrub into a small, carpeted clearing surrounded by patio warmers. In surprised silence, Yelena saw a waiter put the final touches on a full dinner service, complete with white tablecloth and silver.

Oh, my. She glanced up at Alex who was wearing a satisfied smile, then back to the table, her fingers working the gold chain of her necklace.

Alex dismissed the waiter. The man nodded, stepped into a four-wheel drive—another fact she'd failed to register—and slowly drove away into the night.

The clearing gave off seductive heat and light, the air

rife with warm intimacy. When he pulled out her chair she murmured her thanks.

As he sat, Yelena reached for her water glass and took a gulp.

"Carbonara?" Alex offered a dish.

"Thank you." She took the bowl of pasta and spooned some on her plate. "So I talked with Kyle in accounts this afternoon, and I should have final costings tomorrow morning. Cathie, your press officer, has helped with the local side of things and together we're drafting a national release." She picked up her fork. "The sooner we announce it the better, then we can issue the invitations. Can you give me your list first thing tomorrow?"

"Sure."

Yelena blinked, put her fork down and reached for her wineglass. "Thanks again for letting Pam and Chelsea know why I was here."

He nodded, going back to his food. "I thought honesty was best."

Yelena felt a tiny pang and reached for a bread roll, deftly breaking it apart. "Yes." But after she popped the bread in her mouth, she added, "I've also drafted up a six-month plan to coincide with Diamond Falls' anniversary."

Alex slowly lifted his eyes to meet hers. "Can you do me a favor?"

"Yes?"

"Can we not spoil the view by talking about work tonight?"

"Oh." She'd psyched herself up to ask questions: now they all just fizzled on her tongue. "But—"

"Please."

Her skin tingled at that one small word. "Okay."

Perturbed, she concentrated on her food. "This is amazing!" She forked another piece, shoved it in then chewed, rolling her eyes. "I think I'm in love."

Alex chuckled. "Sorry. Franco's already taken."

Yelena gave a melodramatic sigh. "The good ones always are."

Their eyes met casually across the table, both smiling. But when the moment held longer than necessary, Yelena sensed the mood shift gears. This was more than just two people eating dinner. The darkness around them was absolute: it felt as if they were the last two people left on earth. And as Alex studied her over the top of his wineglass, those clear blue eyes slowly took on a darker hue in the dim light.

She quickly stabbed at the pasta.

"Slow down." She heard the humor in his voice. "The food's going nowhere."

"But it's so delicious."

"Speed isn't always best." He placed his fork slowly on the plate, giving her the full blast from his intense eyes. "It's better to savor everything—the taste, the texture—rather than dash through to the end. It can make the rewards so much more—" He paused for deliberate effect, those darkened eyes full of delight "—pleasurable."

She nearly choked. *Dammit.* She tried for a cool stare, but his roguish smile did vaguely illegal things to her body.

Smothering her panic, she dropped her eyes to her plate. Despite the hurt she'd caused him, despite their unrequited fling that had fizzled before it had even started, Alex's intention was crystal clear.

She looked him straight in the eyes. "Did you invite me to dinner to try and seduce me, Alex?"

Her directness didn't faze him. "Do you want me to?"

Her limbs became suddenly lethargic. "No," she lied.

"Why not?" His mouth curled.

Because I don't think I can get over you a second time. "Why would you want to?"

One dark eyebrow lifted. "Answering a question with a question, Yelena?"

She sighed, refolding her napkin to keep her hands occupied. "We hurt each other, Alex. Our past is complicated."

"Yes. But we're here. Now."

He rose with the fluid grace of a dancer, a powerful expanse of potent male. She had to crank her neck up to meet his eyes.

"I'm your PR manager." Nervous now, she, too, stood. But that didn't stop him from encroaching on her personal space.

"Does Bennett & Harper have some morality clause I don't know about?"

How the hell had he gotten so close? His familiar scent tightened her senses, sending subversive shivers over her skin. He smelt of leather, of passion and defiance and warmth. Of losing control. Of Alex.

"Morality clause...?" she choked out. "No."

When his fingers slid slowly between hers, linking them in a shockingly intimate touch, her senses jolted into overdrive.

"See?" He lifted their entwined fingers, his gaze full of secret knowledge. "We have something here."

"It doesn't mean it's right."

"Doesn't mean it's wrong, either."

"Alex..."

She heard the rumble in his throat, just as his eyes briefly closed. "Do you have any idea what my name on your lips does to me?"

And suddenly the time for talking was over.

Alex didn't waste a second on niceties—on the contrary, he took it as if her acquiescence was a given. As if it were his right. And in many ways it was. They'd already been as close as two people could be without actual consummation. And if she were honest with herself, Yelena had missed him. Missed the way his laugh engulfed her like warm flames. Missed his off-beat humor and flirty banter. Missed the feel of his skin against hers. Missed the sensual curve of his mouth and the way it made her want to lose herself, control be damned.

When she leaned in, mouth trembling, a bolt of triumph cleaved into Alex's brain. She wanted him—he'd *made* her want him. Yet in the next instant, white-hot desire saturated every sense, every muscle in his body. He growled, a sound that felt half wild, half uncontrollable, the way she'd always made him feel, and roughly pulled her up against his chest.

She made a small sound but didn't protest, which only fired him up even more. His mouth dipped down, ready to claim hers, but in the last moment, she shoved his chest, her palms hot, knowing she could feel his heart pounding through his shirt.

He stared into her dark eyes, their long lashes heavy with arousal. His blood pounded solidly, breath catching. Did she not want—?

"Let me."

The warm whisper skimming across his mouth did him in. All he wanted to do was rip off her clothes and take her on the ground, surrounded by this raw, primitive backdrop, yet he remained rock still, his groin throbbing with need.

She gently placed her hands at the back of his neck and slid her fingers up through his hair, murmuring appreciatively as she stroked his nape. And as his senses pitched, she pulled his head down.

Her lips brushed his for a second. Then another. She dragged in a breath, almost as if kissing him were somehow painful. But then her eyes opened and a smile spread across her entire face, a smile so full of sensual knowledge that he couldn't help but answer it with one of his own.

Because in the sweetness of her kiss, the pureness she'd given him, he didn't have a hope in hell of keeping his distance. Nothing short of a cyclone could stop him now.

As if sensing the thin line he teetered on, she kissed him again, this time with her eyes wide open, those chocolate-velvet depths reaching in, grabbing what was left of his control and yanking on it, hard.

Yelena felt as if every inch of her skin had completely exploded, that every touch, every smell, every taste was just too much to stand. His arms wrapped her tight up against him, his hard, throbbing maleness jamming into her belly with purposeful intent. The familiar smell of his skin engulfed her, every breath she took filling her up. And the taste…oh, his taste was something she'd always loved. She'd missed that. His mouth covered her bottom lip, gently sucking on the swell. He nibbled, he teased for long, sensual seconds. Then, finally he committed, capturing her mouth and twisting her head into a deep, heart-stopping kiss.

His tongue swept past her lips, teasing hers, encouraging her to respond. So she did, with all the pent-up passion and desire she'd locked away these past months.

Slowly, through the drugging waves of desire, she felt him turn her around and in the next second, the back of her thighs bumped up against the table. Groaning, Alex broke the kiss.

"I always wanted to do this."

And with a grin, he leaned in and cleared the table with one sweep of his arm.

The terrible crash of falling plates and dishes made her gasp, even as a giggle filled her throat.

"I can't wait," he added at her wide eyes.

Her skin flushed hot.

In one easy movement, he cupped her bottom and lifted her onto the table and they kissed again, this time with Alex jammed hard between her thighs. Dazed and drunk from his kisses, she barely felt him unsnap the buttons of her jeans, but when his fingers grazed inside to caress her warmth on the way down, she groaned, hot, demanding desire filling her limbs, her lungs.

He managed to peel both her jeans and knickers off and she gasped as her naked bottom made contact with the cold table. Then his hands were on her knees, caressing her skin beneath warm palms. She shivered.

"Cold?"

She shook her head and his wolfish grin shot her pulse sky-high. That's what she remembered, the way that devilish smile transformed his sculptured face into sin. Desire, so often cloaked in caution, now blazed from his azure eyes.

He studied her, watching her every expression, every tiny movement as his hands continued their excruciatingly slow journey upwards. They stroked her thighs, kneading the muscle beneath her hot skin. First outside, tracing every curve, then slowly, sensuously dipping in to the soft flesh of her inner thighs. When her body quivered in response he chuckled, but still she kept her eyes fixed on his, determined not to break first.

He raised one eyebrow, his look frankly seductive. *Just try it,* her expression said, even as her mouth teased upwards.

Suddenly he fell to his knees, eased her legs apart and the world stopped spinning.

He kissed her inner thigh, his hot breath stirring her curls and eliciting another shiver.

"Relax, Yelena, and enjoy it."

On trembling arms, she leaned back with a groan and gave herself up to the pleasure of pure sensation.

His mouth, warm and insistent, met the most intimate part of her and she jerked, gasping. She'd craved him before, needed his touch so desperately it had hurt. But now, as his tongue skillfully made love to her, every past desire faded into pale comparison.

"Alex…" She heard her half plea, half beg, but felt no shame. His tongue and mouth teased her into a frenzy, building her up with such ridiculous ease she had to bite down on her lip, to hold on to the climax that swelled so close to the surface.

Just when she thought she was doomed, she felt him ease back, his mouth placing gentle kisses along her inner thigh.

She gritted her teeth, groaning her frustration aloud.

He stroked her thighs, nuzzling his chin against her damp skin. "Come for me, Yelena."

All she could do was whimper her acquiescence, her mind whirling with a thousand colors and sensations. Yet she was acutely aware of Alex returning to her, of his skillful tongue as it dipped in and out of her core, his stubbled chin creating rough erotic friction as it rubbed against her hot, sensitive nub.

Her most secret scent surrounded Alex, filling every sense and stoking his lust until he could hardly think straight. Her thighs quivered, he felt her body charge with the sweet release even before he heard her small cry of pleasure.

His groin pressed excruciatingly hard against his fly and he gritted his teeth to force it under control, waiting until Yelena climaxed before he freed himself.

She did, loudly, almost triumphantly. Animal satisfaction charged though his veins, a grunt of victory on his lips. With a final kiss to that sweet flesh on her inner thigh, he swiftly stood and yanked down his jeans.

The picture she presented—leaning back on her elbows, gorgeous face an erotic picture of female satiation as her hair tumbled over one shoulder and down her back—was all it took. Needing no further encouragement, he quickly stepped between her legs, fumbled with the condom packet he'd pulled from his jacket, rolled it on then buried himself in her hot wetness.

Their breath came out in perfect unison, sweet pleasure echoing in the raw, still air.

Spots danced behind his eyes, forcing him to pause, to savor the exquisite, almost painful pleasure of her warmth closing around him. With gritted teeth he waited for control, barely registering that Yelena had removed her top and bra and now lay completely bare for him.

His eyes widened at the sight. Lush curves, defined waist,

breasts a man could lose himself in. He leaned forward, gathering her up and burying his face in the valley between those beautiful mounds. The deep breath he took spun his head.

"Lord, Yelena," he breathed into her skin. "If the world ended tonight, I'd die a happy man."

He felt the laughter rumble through her body, yet when his mouth latched on to one brown erect nipple, she gasped.

He grinned.

"You…" Yelena breathed, before longing obliterated her rebuke. His tongue was now intent on her hard nipple, flicking over and over until she began to squirm.

Inside, he tightened in response.

Oh… Slowly his eyes met hers, now navy with desire. His mouth curled into a smile, partially hidden by the curve of her breast, yet it still had the power to make her wet. Then he left that breast, crossing to the other with no great urgency while inside, she could feel everything build up again.

"Alex, please…"

"Settle," he crooned, placing a hand on her belly as if she was a horse ready to bolt, sending her impatience skyrocketing.

She jerked her hips, squeezing her inner muscles with a soft growl and was rewarded by his tight gasp. Unable to stop herself, she wrapped her arms around his neck, pulled him down and whispered something so outrageously erotic that it stunned even herself.

But it had the desired effect. His groan was pure animal, sending her desire off the charts. He began to move, deep, long thrusts that forced every breath to rush out on the down stroke while every inch of her skin sang with pleasure on the up.

Alex felt the familiar aching joy of orgasm blast him in one almighty wave, only seconds behind Yelena. Every muscle screamed for release as pleasure ripped through him, exploding. He heard a guttural groan in the air, knew it must be his, shocked yet primitively proud to be claiming this moment, this woman, as his.

She moved under him, slick and hot, her nipples pebbling as a cool breeze whispered between them. He reached out, an unsteady hand cupping one breast, warming the cooling flesh.

The moment hung, lengthened, the only sound their mingled breath as heart rates began to slow.

When she shivered, he withdrew, a soft murmur her only reaction.

His withdrawal left Yelena suddenly bereft, the cold air pricking her skin. She quickly reached for her clothes, hearing him do the same.

For some odd reason, her nerves jumped, and not in a good way. As she snapped on her jeans, she heard him flip out his phone, curtly directing his staff to clear away what was left of their meal. All the while, a silent strangeness sat between them. She wanted—needed—to say something more but the words just wouldn't form. She bent to zip up her boots. *Say something. Anything.* Yet the only sound was a lone dingo howling in the distance.

"Yelena."

"Please don't say anything to spoil it, Alex." She zipped up her jacket with stiff fingers, refusing to meet his eyes. She didn't have to see him to know he was frowning. She'd always been astute to his moods—especially irritation.

A moment passed before he said quietly, "Are you ready to go?"

She shoved her hands in her jean pockets and nodded, focusing on the bike and the dry dusty scrub surrounding them—everything but him.

They crunched through the grass and sand in silence. She took the helmet he proffered then swung her leg over the bike, covering a wince as her tender thighs screamed in protest.

As they drove back to Diamond Falls, Yelena allowed herself the guilty luxury of his warmth, his powerful body between her legs. Just like it had been, gloriously hard and naked, pleasuring her not more than ten minutes ago.

Thoughts whirled as the night tore past with cold, sharp fingers. Chemistry they had. But a future? Not when there was too much past between them, so many secrets that weren't hers to reveal.

You can't tell anyone. Not a single soul. For Bella's safety, for Yelena's, Gabriela had sworn her to secrecy. Which meant she couldn't tell Alex the truth. Ever.

She stared off into the night as tears welled then fell down her cheeks before the helmet's thick padding quickly absorbed them.

Nine

The next morning Pam, Alex and Yelena gathered around the conference table in Yelena's office.

Yelena had dressed conservatively in a pair of dark gray pants and a three-quarter-sleeved aqua silk shirt. She'd slicked her hair back, twisting it into an elaborate knot at the base of her neck. Yet every time Alex glanced at her, she might as well have been only wearing underwear the way her skin warmed. And then last night's memories quickly followed, causing every intimate part to tingle and leaving her with an uncomfortable feeling of longing.

Ahh. Last night.

When they'd returned to Diamond Bay, she'd eased off the bike before he'd barely killed the engine and offered a quick "Thank you for dinner" before practically fleeing to her room without a backwards glance.

Thank you for dinner? How lame was she?

Now she pointedly looked away, trying to ignore the

delicious curve of his bottom lip. Lips that had made her climax again and again…

More like, *thank you for rocking my world.*

"Do you want coffee, Yelena?"

She snapped her eyes up to Pam, who had a cup in hand.

"Thank you." She accepted with a smile and took a scalding sip.

Quickly she replaced the cup and drew her notepad forward.

"So I thought we could talk about where we're at with this campaign." She paused, looking at each one in turn before continuing. "We all know the press's direction these last few months. My aim is to turn that around."

"How can you make everyone forget what's been spread in the papers?" Alex asked, one eyebrow raised.

"I can't. We need to focus on the good stuff—charity and community works that will counteract all that gossip."

"You mean we need to suck up."

"No," she said firmly. "I don't want to do anything you'd be uncomfortable with. For example, Pam—" she smiled at Alex's mother "—I love your party idea. In fact, what do you think about calling it the 'Sunset Party'? We could use the gorgeous Outback sunset colors as our signature—red, yellow, dark blue, black—" she refused to falter when her eyes briefly met Alex's "—on decorations and invitations. I have an action plan we can work on together if you'd like."

Pam's face lit up. "I'd be happy to. I also thought we could hire out our boutique clothing for the locals who want to go all out. That way they can dress up but not think we're handing out charity."

Yelena smiled. "That's a great idea. So looking further along—in the next few months it will be slow but steady. One thing I want to address is interviews. Television only, because I can get final edit approval and unlike print, there's less room for misinterpretation. I have contacts with a few stations so I was going to push for *A Current Affair* and—"

"What would we say?" Alex interjected.

Yelena met his combative gaze but before she could answer he added, "Let me rephrase that—what do we *need* to say?"

Yelena leaned back in her chair. "The truth."

His face turned dark. "The public has the truth."

"Not in your own words, it doesn't."

When Alex opened his mouth, Pam interjected, "Yelena's right, Alex. You haven't said anything about—" she hesitated "—that night."

"Mum." Just like that, Alex's anger deflated. "Do you really want to dredge that up again?"

A meaningful look passed between them, one that brought a scowl to Alex's brow and lurched Yelena's burning curiosity into overdrive.

"Leave that with us," Alex finally said in a tone that indicated no further discussion. "What else do you have?"

"Alex." Yelena said firmly, linking her fingers together on the tabletop. "I've been working in PR ever since I left uni, nearly eight years ago. I've had a hand in hundreds of campaigns, from musicians, politicians, doctors and bankers Australia-wide."

"What—"

"Please, let me finish. You chose me because I'm damn good at my job. So can you please trust me to do it?"

She met his silent scrutiny head on, even as her mind suddenly flashed back to last night, to his warm, skillful fingers, his passion-riddled face, the decadent smile as he swooped down for another kiss.

Her skin flared, shocking her. She shook her head, desperate to refocus. "I know it's… difficult sometimes, to open up and reveal things you'd rather keep private. But I need to know you have confidence in me handling this campaign."

"I do," he replied without hesitation.

"So what is it? You're the client," she stressed, determined to cement that fact in her mind. "Do you think I'd do something without your approval?"

"No."

"Then trust me." She slid a list forward, one for each of them. "Here's what I'm going to focus on these next six months. Interviews, yes, but only with reporters I have a standing relationship with." She met Pam's eyes fleetingly. "I can trust these people to be fair and compassionate."

"Really."

Alex's snort of derision irritated her. "Yes. Believe it or not, there are some good guys out there." She nodded to the list and changed tack. "Besides the obvious interviews, there are a few nonofficial things that can subtly boost our profile without taking center stage—*Woman's Weekly* holds an annual Mother's Day shoot, featuring seven high-profile mothers and their children, for example."

Pam looked up and nodded. "I like that."

Encouraged, Yelena smiled.

"'An Australia Day event,'" Alex read. "'Guest spot on *Better Homes and Gardens*'…"

Yelena nodded. "With your solar energy and water recycling, Diamond Falls has an excellent green policy. The public loves the environmental angle, especially from a high-profile business. If you're willing, we can look at a 'give back to the earth' plan, where we can, say, support and fund the reintroduction of native wildlife that's under threat in the area."

"The Gouldian finch," Pam said quickly, naming the tiny, distinctive purple, yellow, green and blue birds. "It's endangered here, as are the golden bandicoot and the loggerhead turtle. I have details and Web sites with more information," she added. "And the Alice Springs Bird Festival runs mid-September, so I'd love to get involved in that somehow."

"I'm sure we can. Thanks, Pam." Instinctively, Yelena knew

she'd hit on something important, something that mattered to Alex's mother. Passion for a cause meant drive, which was always positive.

"'Chelsea fashion magazine intern'?" Alex read from the list.

"Yes. This one has an added bonus," Yelena said. "I know *Dolly*'s senior editor is planning a series of 'dream job' articles starting January, and 'fashion intern' is one of them. A photographer and reporter would follow her around for a day, taking snaps and letting readers know what she does." She looked over at Pam, adding, "Of course, I haven't mentioned this to Chelsea. It's just ideas at the moment and totally subject to approval, of course."

The moment of silence spread, until Pam said slowly, "I think Chelsea would love it."

"What about school?" Alex said.

"She's doing fine with tutors, Alex," Pam assured him.

"Her tennis?"

Pam gave him a long, meaningful look. "She's never wanted to pursue it professionally, darling. And now she has a chance to do something she's truly passionate about."

Alex paused, his expression unreadable. "We should talk about this later," he finally said.

"There's nothing to discuss. I've made up my mind."

Surprise flitted across his face before he shut it down. "Okay."

An odd feeling attached itself to Yelena's skin like remnants of a Band-Aid that refused to disappear even after you ripped the thing off. It continued to stick until their meeting broke up and she finally felt compelled to act.

"Alex? Can I talk with you a moment?"

He nodded, closed the door but remained standing. Nervous, she got to her feet then spent a few seconds silently reworking what she wanted to say in her head.

"I know what you're thinking," Alex finally said.

"Oh?"

"Yeah. And in reply, yes, it was good—no, great. And no, it doesn't have to change anything."

She blinked, startled. "That's not what I was—"

"Yelena, you don't owe me anything," he said shortly. "We haven't exactly promised each other fidelity. Hell," he snorted, a terrible self-derogatory sound. "Given our past, that'd be a stretch anyway."

What? Yelena frowned, her mind whirling with confusion until an awful clarity dawned. He was letting her off the hook for getting pregnant with another man. Worse, he was implying what they had hadn't been all that important anyway. Her heart thudded sickeningly as an awful thought reared up.

It made perfect sense from his perspective.

She swallowed that pain, that dreadful searing hurt he'd delivered with such worldly blasé. *Later. Later, when you're alone.* "Actually, that's not what I wanted to talk to you about. It's your mother."

A frown skittered across his brow. "Why?"

"Do you want to sit?"

"No."

She sighed. "Okay. Look, I think there's something going on with her…" She paused, searching for the right words. "Something she's not saying."

"Like what?"

"Well, it's more of a feeling, a sense I get when we talk." At Alex's narrowed eyes, she added, "For instance, she never mentions your father unless I bring him up. She's not overly affected by all the infidelity accusations. I know he was a brilliant businessman, a self-made man and most are absolute perfectionists."

"Your point?"

Boy, this wasn't any easier even now she'd verbalized it. "Did your parents have a good marriage? Was everything okay?"

He gave her a thorough going-over, eyes astute, hands resting on his hips. Finally he said coolly, "And how is this any of your business?"

She flushed. "I thought—"

"I hired you to do a job, Yelena, not psychoanalyze my family. I'd appreciate you sticking with that. Now if you don't mind, I have a phone conference."

Leaving her openmouthed and cheeks flushed, Alex turned and stalked out the door.

It was over, buried with William Rush. He could not—would not—dig about in the past. It didn't affect just him; it had repercussions for his entire family.

It was better this way, putting Yelena back in her rightful place as his PR consultant. Keeping her focused on her job providing positive spin.

Better, better, better. His feet echoed the chant as he strode down the hall, back to his office. So why did he feel like such a jerk?

He slammed his office door behind him, the sound shaking the walls, reverberating down the hall.

Amongst all the peripheral crap going on in his life, the one constant was his dark, burning need for that woman. Yes, Carlos had betrayed his trust and that would live with him until the day he died. But Yelena… Lord, she'd killed him when she'd disappeared. The one person he thought he could count on, the only one not involved in the media circus of his life and she'd not only wormed her way under his armor but had also taken his trust and ground it into the dirt.

He'd been mentally bereft.

He swung away from the door, towards the expansive view from crystal-clear windows.

His world had been black-and-white, until she'd returned and screaming color had crashed in. Yet he couldn't surrender that power again. He couldn't afford the devastation it would leave in its wake.

* * *

Yelena was grateful for the sudden frantic work load of the upcoming party—it meant she could claim to be legitimately busy and not think about what had transpired these last few days. And Alex must have felt the same way, judging by the way he pointedly avoided being alone with her.

Even though he'd declared their past a nonissue, Yelena could feel the ghosts dog her every moment from that point on. It made talking business awkward, it made every movement calculated so she didn't accidentally touch him. So incredibly exasperating when all she *wanted* to do was touch him.

Even as her efforts began to snowball into a solid campaign, she was still relieved when six o'clock rolled around and she could spend time with her daughter. Chelsea had taken to dropping by every night and Yelena gratefully welcomed the company and her obvious attentiveness to Bella. To her delight Pam turned up on Friday night and they all spent a pleasant evening watching television and eating dinner.

When Yelena's phone rang, she was midlaugh at something Chelsea had said. It was Jonathon, calling to approve her request to stay another week. But in the course of that brief exchange, Yelena sensed something was off. His next words confirmed it. When she hung up, her good mood evaporated.

"Problem?" Pam asked, her legs curled elegantly beneath her on the sofa.

"Just work. Can you keep an ear out for Bella? I need to see Alex about something."

Yelena grabbed her room card and strode out the door, oblivious to the look Pam and Chelsea exchanged as edginess began to swirl swiftly in her belly.

She knocked on Alex's door and after a moment it swung open. Before he could say a word, she swept past him then pivoted in the middle of the room, arms crossed.

"I just got a call from my boss," she started without preamble.

He scratched his chin, a harsh yet intimate sound in the warm room. "You're going to have to elaborate here."

"Did you tell him that we're romantically involved?"

"No."

"You sure?"

"Yelena, I've not spoken with the man for nearly a week."

He tipped his head, hands on his hips. It was then Yelena finally noticed his clothes...or rather, lack of them. His white shirt, unbuttoned and rumpled, teased open to reveal the curves and planes of a magnificent torso. Her eyes trailed slowly down, skimming over his chest to his stomach. His muscles were a work of finest sculpture, chiseled and touchable under warm, tanned skin, before tapering down to slim hips encased in black pants, belt suggestively unbuckled.

Too late she snapped her eyes up to his, the full body flush warming every inch of her skin.

"Finished looking?" His voice was husky, his eyes amused.

Her body hummed with energy, as if she'd stuck her finger in a light socket and the powerful force now thrashed to break free.

"I..." She paused, struggling for the upper hand. "So if it wasn't you, who?"

He shrugged. "Who else knows you're here?"

A spark of irritation nipped at the edges of desire. "My father. Carlos."

He didn't have to say a thing, his expression mirrored her thoughts. Carlos wouldn't. Her father, on the other hand, was Jonathon's squash partner.

Contrite and embarrassed, she broke eye contact. "I...I'm sorry. I may have jumped the gun."

"Not a problem."

She glanced back up and caught his smile at the worst possible moment. Now all she could think about were those curved lips nipping at her hot skin.

"Okay. Er..." She clasped her hands nervously in front of her body. "I'd better be—" she gestured one thumb over her shoulder, towards the door "—better be going."

"Okay."

Still she remained rooted to the spot, until Alex added helpfully, "Anything else?"

"Yes. No! No, I'll..." With a whoosh of breath she whirled to the door. *Estúpida. Surely you're not waiting for an invitation into his bed?*

She paused, her hand on the door handle, her back to him. Thanks to what would've undoubtedly been a skillful, off-the-cuff comment, her father had effectively undermined her and cast doubt on her abilities, reducing her to fifteen all over again, and with all the accompanying emotions of confusion, isolation and anger.

The same emotions Alex himself had dealt with on a daily basis since his father's death. Without her.

"I'm sorry, Alex."

"For what?"

She squeezed her eyes shut. "For not being there for you when your father died."

She paused, waiting, but his silence said it all. With a pained frown she cracked open the door, prepared to make a dignified exit.

It happened so suddenly she barely got out a squeak of surprise. One moment she was grasping the handle, the next Alex had slammed it shut, grabbed her arms and whirled her, pinning her up against the door.

He was in her personal space, close enough she could see the dark navy flecks in his eyes and the rough stubble on his strong chin, feel his warm breath brushing her cheek.

Then he kissed her, hard.

Their breath mingled, tongues tangling until her nipples pebbled in painful arousal beneath her shirt. His manhood pushed hard against her belly and when she shifted, his groan was a mix of vexation and desire.

She felt it, too, this fierce need that scorched like a fever under her skin, her willpower bending and swaying under its awesome power. Her mind tangled as she felt his hands under her shirt, slide up over her waist then her ribs, before he cupped her breasts.

His soft murmur of approval in her mouth fired her blood, sending aching shards of longing into her limbs, fanning across her body.

He fiddled with her bra clasp as they kept on kissing, and when her bra fell free, he bunched up her shirt and latched hot mouth on to one tight nipple.

"Alex…" A groan of pleasure ripped from deep within as her legs began to buckle.

"I have you," he murmured, his lips full of her flesh. It was true—his arms wrapped securely around her, the hard door at her back. His knee wedged between her legs, offering erotic support.

He was everywhere, in her senses, her mind, under her skin. In her blood. She took a breath and he was there. She opened her eyes and his face filled her vision. Her palms, shaking with passion, ran over his shoulders, until she cupped his nape, that special erotic area where his hair met vulnerable flesh.

It turned her on every time. She tunneled her fingers in his hair, gently pulling, a deep burst of satisfaction as she heard him grunt. Yet despite the raging desire in her blood and her desperation to have him inside her, she couldn't relinquish herself. Not tonight. Not now.

"Alex…" she whispered, desperate to ignore the shocks of pleasure as his tongue ran over her nipple, teasing and arousing it to painful erection. "I need to gooooooo…" Her plea ended on a groan as his hand dipped into her pants, his fingers quickly finding the damp sensitive nub of her arousal.

"Do you?" His teeth toyed with one rock-hard nipple, making her hiss.

"Your…mother and Chelsea….are….with—" his tiny strokes made her body jerk with pleasure; she squeezed her eyes shut, forcing her body to settle even as it screamed in joy "—Bella. We can't do this right now."

His hand stilled and Yelena breathed a sigh. Relief or disappointment? Right now, she had no idea.

Slowly, he lifted his head and Yelena nearly lost it then—the fire in his eyes still raged, bathing her in desperate yearning. His hand was still down the front of her pants, his fingers wedged intimately in her flesh, flesh that throbbed and ached beneath his touch.

"I need to go," she repeated breathlessly.

The moments ticked into seconds, long, apprehensive seconds that did nothing to clear the passion-fueled moment. Yet Alex finally gave in. In one slow, excruciating movement, he slid from her, the sensual glide of his fingers forcing her to swallow a frustrated groan.

Then the cool air rushed in. She opened her eyes just in time to see his jaw tighten before he turned away, tunneling fingers through his hair.

Abject disappointment warred with common sense. "Alex…"

"Don't." He got out hoarsely, his back still to her. "You need to go."

She blinked, still dazed. Then without another word she opened the door and finally escaped.

Alex whirled to the closed door, a deep scowl across his brow. Gently he thumped a clenched fist on his forehead, one hand on his hip. His groin throbbed, a painful reminder of what he'd had, what he still wanted. Yelena.

He muttered a few choice curses under his breath before

yanking his shirt free from his pants. This wasn't him, unable to figure out the simplest of problems. He'd had a mission—destroy Carlos's world by sleeping with his precious sister. But instead of triumph, bitterness tainted his every move, his every thought. Even when he thought about how amazing Yelena had felt in his arms, how mind-blowing it had been to finally taste her, to kiss her, to be inside her, a surge of guilt always followed.

Something he hadn't felt in a long, long time.

He'd used her in his revenge plan, even though he'd never been certain it'd work, even though he'd begun to believe she hadn't played a part in Carlos's lies.

The kicker was she had no idea how much of a bastard Carlos was.

The injustice of it burned like fire as he strode into the kitchen, wrenched open the fridge door and grabbed a beer. He scowled at nothing in particular, until his gaze landed on Yelena's file for the Sunset Party. He still hadn't given her his guest list—

It hit him like a bolt from heaven, immobilizing every muscle in his body. With a rush of breath that ended on a stunned grunt, he slammed a hand on the counter top.

If Yelena couldn't see the kind of person Carlos was, then it was up to him to *show* her. And he knew just the thing.

Ten

Saturday morning—the day of the party—slowly blended into early afternoon. After fussing over her hair, her makeup and her general nerves, Yelena walked into her lounge room for Chelsea's inspection.

"How do I look?"

Chelsea frowned, gently replacing Bella across her other shoulder. "As if you're about to chair a board meeting." The teenager looked fabulous in a sleek, dark blue halter neck, the empire waist slashed to reveal aqua-and-black satin that shimmered as she walked.

"What's wrong with this?" Yelena ran a hand down her red silk shirt then readjusted the waistband of the black wool pencil skirt.

"It's hardly a party dress, is it?"

"Well, I'm working."

"You're always working." Chelsea rolled her eyes. "It's a *party,* for heaven's sakes. You know—food, people, music?"

She sighed melodramatically. "Okay, you'd better let me look at what you've got."

In less than ten minutes, Chelsea declared every piece of clothing in Yelena's lineup unsuitable and was on the phone. Three minutes, to the dot, and the concierge was at her door with a special delivery.

"Open it," Chelsea commanded after she'd signed the slip and closed the door. To Yelena's surprise, a scorching-red dress unfurled beneath her hands.

"Go and try it on."

"I can't—"

"Yeah, you can," Chelsea countered firmly, hands on hips.

Yelena finally caved. "All right. Can you watch Bella?"

"Sure. And loosen up that hair!" Chelsea added as she went once more into the bedroom.

Yelena pulled on the delicious dress, the fabric pouring over her skin with silken cool fingers. She couldn't suppress a shiver of excitement as she stared at her reflection.

It was one of the most gorgeous gowns she'd ever seen. Stylish, dramatic and totally sexy. The strapless bodice hugged her figure to snug perfection, the sleek material emphasizing her waist and generous curves to flare past her hips into an elegant, floor-length train. A swathe of sheer red floated behind her, a flirty mermaid tail with tiny seeded crystals on the hem to add extra oomph when she walked.

There was a small knock on the door before Chelsea opened it a crack.

"Mum's here. Come on out and show—wow!" Chelsea's eyes widened. But her smile faltered when she came to Yelena's hair. "Hair down. Fluff it out."

"Yes, miss." Yelena grinned and reached for the pins holding it in place. It tumbled down, the soft whisper across her bare shoulders sending another shiver down her spine. "You know, Gabriela used to boss me about like that, too."

Sadness flittered across Chelsea's eyes before she smiled. "Well, she *did* have style." She eyed Yelena before adding, "And you have awesome hair—why on earth would you tie it up all the time?"

Yelena grinned at her though the mirror. "Try living with it."

"Pleeeease." Chelsea tweaked Yelena's curls into place, smoothed her own shiny, straight hair behind her ears then nodded at their reflections. "Okay. Let's go."

When Yelena swished into the lounge room, Alex stood there, talking in hushed whispers with Pam who was holding Bella. Alex and she had barely spent an hour together since that kiss. Yelena had been gratefully busy with the party preparations and via Chelsea, she'd gleaned that Alex was dealing with the day-to-day running of his father's businesses.

Yet when he glanced up, saw her and smiled, her normally iron composure just crumbled.

"You look gorgeous." His eyes told her much more, all of it definitely X-rated, judging by the glint in those jeweled depths.

"Thanks" was all she could choke out, more than aware of his sister and mother standing discreetly to the side, Chelsea attempting to fasten a simple gold necklace around Pam's neck as Bella gurgled.

"I didn't think a ball gown would've been on your packing list."

"The dress is yours, bro," Chelsea piped up, too focused on pretending not to listen to actually carry it off. "Lori at the boutique gave me a loaner."

Yelena met his eyes head-on, a small smile hovering over her lips as she shrugged.

"Nice," he murmured. But the timbre in that one word said so much more. Like, *I'd much prefer you out of it.*

Even as her body leaped in response, she gave him a steady

glare, telling him she knew exactly where his mind was at. He remained unfazed.

Just as Alex was about to offer his arm, Yelena took Bella from Pam.

"You're bringing her?" he asked, surprised.

Yelena shot him a cool look. "It's her first party. I have Jasmine coming over at six."

He eyed the gurgling baby, sitting comfortably on Yelena's hip. "Won't she—"

"What?"

"I don't know—throw up or something?"

Yelena laughed. "Maybe."

"What about your dress?"

"Then it'll get dirty."

Her smile stretched as the women shared the joke, one that made him feel uncomfortably male.

"Yelena's letting me show Bella off." Pam finally came to her son's rescue. "And after the wonderful job she's done, we can at least give her a dress."

"It's not that," he began, glancing at his mother. She was looking chic in a black pantsuit, a burnt-orange wrap around her shoulders. When she smiled, it was a real one, not those fake smiles that never reached her eyes, ones he'd seen her give way too often when his father was still alive.

They opened the door, Pam and Chelsea going first in a rush of excited whispers.

"My earrings!" Yelena said suddenly. Then to Alex, "Can you hold Bella?" and just like that, the baby was suddenly in his arms.

God, she was so tiny! He blinked, awkwardly clutching her to his chest like an oddly shaped piece of delicate china. Bella gurgled and gnawed on one fist, a thin line of drool slowly dripping from her mouth.

He shifted her minuscule, yellow-jumpsuited weight and studied her with a frown. Large, brown puppy-dog eyes fringed with thick lashes stared up from a round, cherubic face. Abundant, curly dark hair capped her head, her tiny mouth stretching into a wide grin, still full of baby fist and drool.

She was a miniature version of Yelena.

Something fluttered inside, making his breath catch, prompting a darker frown. Yet when Bella kept grinning at him and two tiny dimples appeared on the baby's cheeks, his heart skipped a beat.

The sight that greeted Yelena's return stopped her in her tracks, stuttering her breath. Alex cradled a tiny gurgling Bella in his powerful arms. And they were grinning at each other.

Oh, my Lord. The perfect picture sent a slice of yearning into her very soul, her heartbeat engulfing her heavy swallow. She blinked. *What am I supposed to do with that?*

"Alex?"

When his eyes swung to hers she nearly crumpled at the dazed expression there. A mixture of awe, delight... and something else, something she recognized but did not want to name because then she'd have to acknowledge it. And worse, deal with it.

Longing. Her conscience overrode common sense at the worst possible moment.

She dropped eye contact and reached for Bella. "Pam and Chelsea are waiting. Shall we go?"

But when he remained still, staring at her with Bella still in his arms, a spurt of panic erupted.

"Alex?" Yelena said softly.

Inscrutable eyes studied her, as if he wanted nothing more than to crawl into her mind and read her thoughts. She returned his gaze steadily, unblinkingly, even as her whole body inwardly trembled.

"She could have been ours."

No bitterness, no accusation. Yet the pure simplicity of his statement made every cell in her body weep.

Anguish threatened her composure: ruthlessly she choked it down. "I know."

He sighed, severing the moment as he firmly handed Bella over. "Let's go."

For a week, construction on two marquees had been underway, and now the results of everyone's hard work was clearly visible. Inside the main entrance, fake trees sparkled with tiny lights and a canopy of dark blue silk dotted with tiny diamantés gave a starry effect. A small pond and miniature waterfall had been built and, surrounding it sat massive toadstools with assorted fake bugs and critters as big as cats. Children squealed and shrieked and adults gasped as they discovered replicas of popular Aboriginal folklore creatures scattered amongst the scenes—a platypus in the pond, an emu grazing behind a tree. Koalas hid in the branches and kangaroos grazed lazily on the long painted scrub.

The back of this scene opened up to a huge, carpeted area, where long trestle tables were laden with a veritable feast, the local cuisine mixed in with Diamond Bay's offerings. Chelsea had dubbed this area the 'party tent,' where a bunch of local bands were setting up their equipment.

As Yelena watched the flow of guests arrive, she realized most of the small but fiercely strong community had turned up.

Which hopefully meant it was going to be a roaring success.

To her right, at the back of the marquee, her daughter commanded the attention of a handful of women. She chuckled, watching the way Chelsea kept on touching Bella's hand, how Pam gently patted her back. A baby had an amazing ability to bring out women's mothering instincts.

Most, that is, except Maria Valero's.

She blinked, burying that thought away. Now was not the time to dwell on things she couldn't change.

She glanced over at two reporters filming their segment

intros. The press was here; the guests were arriving. With a smile she watched a bunch of excited Aboriginal children run full tilt through the marquee, laughing as their squeals of delight filtered outside.

"Looks like it's going to be a hit."

She nearly jumped out of her skin as Alex's seductive breath washed over her shoulder.

She swiveled to meet his eyes. "You doubted my skills?"

His smile spread slowly, creasing his eyes in mischievous glee. "Not in the least."

As they exchanged a silent look she sensed a ground shift. As if something had changed in some deep, profound way.

"We're talking about the party, right?" she said slowly, her eyes flitting back towards the arriving throng.

"Of course."

She avoided his gaze, nervously pressing one hand to her abdomen before flicking a long curl over her shoulder. It obviously proved too much of a temptation because Alex retrieved it, twirling it around his finger in deep concentration.

The look in his bright blue eyes made her knees buckle. "You'd..." She swallowed and tried again. "You'd better go and attend to your guests."

His mouth spread into a grin. Then to her astonishment he took her hand, kissed it and bowed low like a gallant courtier. "Of course. I'll be back."

Yelena watched him go, smiling as guests continued to arrive. Pam mingled with natural ease, talking to employees and their families, local business owners, even Yelena's contacts from Sydney and Canberra.

She spotted Chelsea shyly chatting to the waiter who had caught her eye a few days ago and her smile widened.

Then a broad figure cut through the crowd and that smile froze in place.

"Carlos!"

* * *

From his vantage point across the room, Alex watched his enemy greet Yelena with a smile and a hug. Yelena's obvious joy at her brother's presence sliced Alex's insides. But his veins iced over when he caught Carlos's complacent smirk, a look that said he knew and fully accepted his sister's worship as his God-given right.

Yelena's eyes sought his, yet he met her curiosity with a raised eyebrow and a shrug. The grateful smile she shot him dug in the knife just a little more.

She won't thank you after tonight.

Swallowing that bitter pill, he grimly reconnoitered and moved forward.

"What are you doing here?"

He heard Yelena's happy exclamation then saw her brother's mouth curve. Yet those dark eyes remained wide and alert. "Is that any way to talk to one of your guests, *cigüeñita?*"

Her smile faltered. The nickname "little stork" had annoyed her ever since tenth grade, but her irritation only amused Carlos.

"I got an invite in the mail. I would've expected at least a phone call," Carlos said casually as she grabbed him a drink from a passing waiter. The gentle yet obvious rebuke wrinkled Yelena's brow.

He took a gulp of his drink, gagged then choked it down. "What the—?"

"Iced tea. Yandurruh is an alcohol-free community."

"Great. Another reason why I hate the Outback."

That was Alex's cue. He stepped up behind them. "We have a fully stocked bar at Diamond Bay if you prefer, Carlos."

"Alex." Carlos slowly turned and they both went through the motions of shaking hands.

Yelena glanced from one man to the other, studying them closely. They were both tall and strikingly good-looking. But where Carlos had that Antonio Banderas, swarthy-romantic-screen-idol look, Alex's appeal was infinitely more subtle. From his short-cropped hair to the strong, stubbled jaw and piercing blue eyes, his appearance reminded her of powers barely leashed, of treacherous waters lurking beneath his cool, controlled exterior.

Seeing them together was palpably uncomfortable to watch, like witnessing two rival politicians exchange pleasantries just before they ripped each other to shreds.

"I'd kill for a real drink," Carlos said gruffly as they broke the handshake.

Yelena winced at his word choice, noticing the dark clouds passing over Alex's face.

"I'll show you the way," she said quickly, linking her arm in his. As they walked away, she chanced a backwards glance.

Pam and Chelsea had joined Alex and as she watched, Alex's gaze landed on Bella.

His mouth curled up, his finger going out to stroke the baby's soft cheek.

Carlos frowned down at her. "You all right?"

She nodded, releasing her tight grip on his arm. He glanced back and his frown deepened.

They silently made their way through the night until they reached the security gate that signaled the perimeter of Diamond Bay property. Yelena keyed open the gate and led Carlos through.

"Nice place," Carlos mused as they followed the path through the lush vegetation. "Must've cost billions to develop."

Yelena ground to a halt, forcing Carlos to stop, too. "Tell me what happened, Carlos."

"About...?"

"Between you and Alex. You were business partners. You were *friends*. And now—"

"What's *he* said?" Carlos efficiently flicked a small leaf from his sharp collar.

"Nothing. He refuses to talk about it."

"I'm not surprised."

"What's that supposed to mean?"

Carlos raised one perfect eyebrow before turning back to the path. With a growl of annoyance, Yelena followed.

"Well, look who his father is—a man who went from poverty to topping Australia's rich list. Of course he's not going to tell you he screwed up."

They finally reached the sweeping courtyard of Merlot, Diamond Bay's most popular wine bar.

Yelena grabbed his sleeve, bringing him to a halt. "What do you mean, 'screwed up'?"

Carlos sighed and crossed his arms. "Sprint Travel isn't doing well."

What? Why hadn't Alex told her? "How? Management? Capital? Advertising?"

"Lots of things I won't get into." *It's over your head so don't worry about it,* his look said. Yelena's eyebrows ratcheted up at the barely veiled insult. "I'll have to take it to the courts."

"You're going to *fight* him for the company?"

"I'm surprised you don't know this, considering all you're doing for him." His expression tightened before quickly smoothing out. "I have no choice," he added matter-of-factly. "Sprint Travel can't survive with Alex Rush at the helm." He gave her arm a pat for good measure. "And Alex will do anything to get the upper hand with the business. Including—" he dropped his gaze, unable to meet her eyes "—using you to get to me."

"What's that supposed to mean?"

Carlos gave her a hurt look. "I'm just looking out for you, Yelena. I've dealt with men like Alex before. He'll stop at nothing to get what they want. Now, are you coming in for a drink?"

She shook her head slowly, then watched Carlos shrug, pity and regret on his handsome face. That couldn't be right.

Alex wasn't like that. And he wouldn't withhold that kind of information.

The realization that this was much bigger than she'd first thought lay like fiery leaden chains across her chest. It followed her as she left Carlos and went back to the party, dogged her steps as she put on her happy face and mingled with the guests while she looked for Alex.

She found him in front of a camera, being interviewed for a national news channel. On first glance he appeared relaxed and confident with one hand in his pocket, one gesturing as he talked. Yet even from this distance she could tell he was out of his comfort zone: the rigid jaw and shoulders, for one. The small tight lines around his mouth. Even his casual, wide-legged stance. The body language in all his press footage said the same thing: "I'd rather be somewhere else."

"…one final question, Mr. Rush," the female presenter was saying. "How are you coping now, nine months on from your acquittal of your father's death?"

Every muscle in his body appeared to stiffen. His hands clenched, eyes narrowing to forbidding slits.

Yelena stepped forward. "Hello, Val. You *do* know a person can't be acquitted for something they were never charged with?" She casually glanced around. "I thought Mark was on this piece."

Val Marchetta shrugged her thin shoulders and tilted her head, an affected gesture meant to encourage confidences. "They sent me instead. Fancy seeing you here, Yelena." The icy smile mirrored in her wide, perfectly made-up eyes.

"Yes. Excuse me," she said, smiling politely. "Alex, could I see you for a moment?"

She took his arm, smiled again at the now-frowning Val then firmly led him away.

"You didn't have to rescue me," he said tightly as they kept on walking.

"Just think of it as preempting a possible awkward moment."

She threw a brief glance back over her shoulder. "And when Val puts the pieces together, our business relationship will no longer be private."

Alex shrugged. "It had to happen eventually."

They were finally outside, pausing in a corner where brief shadows gently merged, cooling the early evening. The dozen questions teetering on her tongue all dissolved into a soft murmur of surprise when Alex swiftly pulled her into his arms and kissed her.

Purpose immediately melted into divine pleasure. His hands held her face, trapping her mouth in a sensual prison and with a half sigh, half groan, she kissed him back.

For minutes they indulged in the simple, erotic pleasure of sharing mouths and tongues, oblivious to the party in full swing inside, to the people walking and mingling not two meters away. Minutes in which Yelena forgot what she'd marched over to say, forgot her exchange with Carlos...hell, she even forgot her name at one point.

When Alex finally broke the kiss, they were both breathless and heavy eyed.

"Do you want to leave?" he asked, voice husky.

"I can't."

"I didn't ask if you could. I asked if you wanted to."

More than you know. "Alex, I'm working. Did you talk to the press—the *other* press?" she added.

He sighed. "I did. So did Pam."

"No hiccups? Everything's going smoothly?"

"From what I can see." But at her look, he paused. "Except..?"

"Carlos."

"Ahh." Slowly he released her and took a step back, shoving his hands into his pockets.

"Did you invite him?"

"Yes."

"Why?"

To show you how manipulative and selfish he is. "Because I know how much he means to you."

The look on her face was inscrutable. "He's been making accusations."

"About?"

"Sprint Travel's on the rocks."

"It is," he said slowly.

She sucked in a breath. "You're paying a small fortune for B&H to represent you and you fail to tell me this? Are you crazy? Or do you really not care what I'm trying to do here?"

Alex's expression tightened. "It's complicated."

"Oh, how I wish people would stop telling me that! This is why you and Carlos had a falling out, right?"

"Yes."

"But—" she crossed her arms "—that's not all."

Alex seesawed between two truths while his gut pitched. He wanted her to *see* the real Carlos, not just tell her. Why should she believe him over her flesh-and-blood brother?

"It's—"

"Complicated. Right."

This was not going well.

"If you could just give me some time to—"

"Was the other night just a way to get back at my brother?"

He had to hand it to her, she had style. She delivered that question so calmly she could've been inquiring about the weather. Impassive face, straight back. Yet through the businesslike façade, Alex knew he'd hurt her.

Damn. "Yelena." He moved to take her hand but she just stepped back, one eyebrow raised. He squelched a frown, guilty as hell. "That night, it was just you and me. I was thinking of nothing else, had no ulterior motive except pleasure. Yours and mine."

He'd never wanted someone to believe him more at this

moment. Even after all those months of speculation and repeated interrogation by the cops, Yelena's belief meant everything right now.

"You didn't answer my question."

For one stupid, insane moment it was revenge. Not now. He couldn't meet her eyes, couldn't bear to see the hurt in those wide depths. A disgusted murmur echoed in his throat, self-loathing rising up to choke him.

As the silence and growing distance thundered between them, the cheerful sounds of the party breezed by on the cooling air, paradoxically highlighting the moment with almost vulgar emphasis.

His tongue refused to work, words sticking inside his mouth. Yet at her raised eyebrow, he finally settled on "I didn't mean to hurt you."

"Really?" she got out, her frosty look now glacial. "Wow. Imagine if you tried."

"Yelena—"

"Don't, Alex. I can't…" She shook her head firmly. "I need to feed Bella and put her to bed."

Then she was gone.

Eleven

On swift, urgent feet, Yelena clicked into the main marquee, yet just as she was about to enter, a jagged sob caught her throat.

Mortified, she quickly stepped back, swallowing that horrible vulnerability down. *You can't cry. Not here, not now.*

Sheer willpower forced back the tears, sent steel into her composure and determination into every muscle. With a quick toss of her head she stepped inside.

It took under a minute to find her daughter, the center of attention in a bunch of cooing women. Despite her swirling thoughts, Yelena managed a smile. Pam had Bella cradled securely over her shoulder, doing that familiar, slow step-sway dance every mother did to comfort a baby.

She moved forward.

"It's getting close to six—time to feed Bella," she said, careful to ensure Pam knew she was there before putting a hand on the woman's shoulder.

Pam turned and smiled. "I hope you're coming back to the party."

Yelena nodded. "I'll see how it goes. The staff seem to have things under control."

A movement caught her eye and Yelena glanced across. Alex stood at the exit.

Their eyes met and despite the horrible truth she now knew, Yelena felt every nerve in her body charge.

"Yelena?"

"Mmm?"

"I can take Bella if you want."

Yelena took a deep breath and refocused on Pam. "I'm sorry?"

The older woman was smiling in a way that Yelena couldn't fail to interpret. "I can go and put Bella down if you want to—that is, I mean…"

Now they were both embarrassed. "No, that's okay," Yelena assured her, her skin flushing with guilt. "She's been a bit fussy. Unfamiliar surroundings, I think."

She gently extricated Bella with a smile then made her way outside.

Alex was nowhere to be seen. Yelena sighed. *Relieved? Or disappointed?*

Both. She keyed open the security gate and soon the gardens engulfed her.

With a shiver, she quickly made her way down the winding path, lush foliage and the sounds of dusk whispering around her. The afternoon heat had eased off as the ritual preparation for sunset began. Thanks to enthusiastic discussions with Pam, she recognized a flock of rare Princess parrots noisily roosting in River Red Gums, then farther on, more busy bird chatter in the spinifex grass. The trees and plants were abundant, providing coverage for not only the bird population but also various reptiles she'd spotted most mornings soaking up the sun on her patio.

Lost in the sights and sounds, she started when she rounded the curve and Carlos emerged from the opposite direction.

She gave him a smile, too tired to make sure she meant it. "Having a good time?"

She waited while he lazily took a drag of his cigarette before blowing smoke into the air.

Her smile dropped as she pointedly coughed then repositioned Bella on her other shoulder.

"Not as much as you are, apparently."

Her mouth thinned but she said nothing.

"He denied trying to take Sprint Travel then," Carlos said flatly.

"I didn't ask him."

"Oh, right. Too busy, were you?"

She sniffed, catching the scent of scotch on his breath, but clamped her mouth shut, smiling politely as she made way for a passing couple.

"The man isn't fit to run a charity raffle," Carlos said, grinding the cigarette beneath his toe. "And you're cheapening yourself hanging around him."

Her breath came in sharp. "What?"

"Just look at his family. His father grew up in Bankstown, for starters," he scoffed.

"So did Paul Keating, Australia's twenty-fourth prime minister. What does living in Sydney's western suburbs prove?"

Carlos sighed. "Breeding, Yelena. William Rush cheated on his wife. Then he dies in mysterious circumstances and Alex gets off scot-free. And from what I'm hearing, Rush Airlines' business practices weren't exactly aboveboard."

Yelena shook her head. "That's the first I'm hearing of it."

"Well." Carlos glanced past her, his smile hinting at condescension. "I have sources. If you stood to inherit a billion-dollar company and knew it was going down the gurgler, wouldn't you be a little pissed off?"

"I'm not going to validate that by answering."

He swung his gaze back to her, eyes blazing. "You're a Valero. What you do is public business and reflects on everyone, especially Papá. I think he'd have something to say about what is going on here."

A cold shard iced over her heart. "Carlos…"

"And for heaven's sakes, Yelena, fix your hair! It looks like you've just tumbled from his bed."

Yelena automatically put her hand to her head as he glanced about again.

Then she stilled. Slowly, she let her hand fall.

Carlos's narrowed eyes caught that. "I thought at least *you'd* have a little restraint. I knew Gabriela was a bad influence."

She sucked in a breath. "Do not say *one* word against our sister." Now she just itched to slap him. But frankly, she wouldn't give him the satisfaction of seeing her lose control.

"Well, what would you call it? First, thanks to her we end up in this god-awful, ass-end-of-the-world country! Then she becomes a discount store *model*—" he spat out the word like others would say "prostitute" "—then she calls and you drop everything to bum around Europe for months on end. God knows what you both ended up doing over there."

"Remember, she died, Carlos," Yelena choked out.

His eyes barely rested on Bella before he glanced away. "And you end up with a bastard child."

The air crackled with rising tension and Yelena tried to shove her way through it. But his bitter expression, one that went beyond mere anger and disappointment, forced a terrible thought into her brain.

"And you'll never forgive me for that, will you?" she said slowly. His impatient gesture told her what he thought of that ridiculous thought. But gradually, clarity began to dawn. "Here, hold your niece."

"Hey!" Carlos took a step back, hands up, and in that moment, Yelena saw a brief flash of disgust twist across his face. It shattered something inside her, propelling a bitter acrid burn into her throat.

"Oh, my God," she whispered fiercely. "You can't even hold her, can you?"

Carlos plastered on a tight smile, nodding politely as a woman walked past.

"What are you talking about?" he finally hissed.

"You've never once picked her up, talked to her, engaged with her. She's a *baby,* Carlos. And just because I don't have a husband does not give you the right to—"

"To what?" he spat, the venom pitched low and hard as he grabbed Yelena's arm. "We are Valeros, descended from Spanish royalty! *Dios,* the irony from you, a public relations expert." He dropped her arm with a snort of disgust. "Did you think for one second how this looks for our father? Our mother? You're not only flaunting that child but you're also sleeping with a convict, a man who killed his father!"

"He did not kill anyone!" Yelena countered, gently patting Bella as she stirred.

"Oh, and you were there, were you?"

"Yes, I was."

Triumph leaked from her voice: she felt it empower every muscle, every bone as she lifted her chin.

Carlos stepped back, a dark frown contorting his face. "You weren't."

"Alex was with me at the time his father died. Let it go, Carlos."

He looked so stunned that for one second, Yelena almost took pity on him. Yet she knew, really knew, how he felt about her and Bella and she just couldn't forgive him for that.

Carlos might be family, but so was Bella. She glanced

down at her sleeping baby, cupping her warm head with one trembling hand. Carlos not only treated her presence like dirt under his triple-stitched, imported Spanish shoes but now this… this.. disgusting revelation.

All that history had been stripped away, reduced to nothing but bitter ashes. Carlos had done that.

"I don't want to argue, Carlos," she muttered, exhaustion and loss engulfing her.

"Then don't." He gave her a tight look. "I'm going back to the bar."

Yelena watched him stalk off without a word, her heart aching. Carlos was her brother. Her charming, funny, smart brother, her champion, her protector. She'd worshipped him. He was her flesh and blood. He and Gabriela were family, more than her absent parents ever were.

When had it all gone sour?

On quick footsteps she got to her suite, smiled at the waiting Jasmine then keyed them both in. She prepared the formula then went into the bedroom, settling in the comfy rocking chair and positioned Bella in her arms.

As Bella fed, the insistent pounding that had settled in the middle of her forehead slowly began to ease. Yet she refused to think about what had just happened, not until she'd settled the baby. Instead she sighed, releasing the tension from her tight shoulders, let the moment calm her limbs and relax her body as she watched Bella feed.

Too soon, the formula was gone and Bella's eyes had fluttered closed. After a moment, Yelena rose then gently tucked her into the crib. Staring down at that sweet, innocent face, her heart tightened just a little more.

Carlos's disapproval had always been there, she acknowledged as her hand rested gently on Bella's rising chest. After moving to Australia, Gabriela had curbed her rebellion into small localized ones. Hair, makeup, wardrobe and boyfriends were the main points of contention. And when she'd reached eighteen, her brief fling with modeling had earned her enough money to move out.

Despite the years in between, guilt still burned.

What Gabriela didn't know was the more waves she caused, the more Yelena deliberately smoothed them. Controlling her environment, bringing order into her disorganized world, like Alex had said.

With one last look at her now-sleeping daughter, she crept from the room.

"Going back to the party?" Jasmine asked, glancing up from the book she'd been reading.

Yelena nodded, unable to force out pleasantries. Swiftly she picked up her purse and quietly left.

She couldn't let it go like this.

A myriad of conflicting emotions dogged every step as she walked down the shadowed path, twisting and turning inside. It hurt, damn, it hurt. It was her *brother,* the same man who'd said all those awful things, shown her a terrible side she'd never witnessed before.

But if she gave up on Carlos, she'd have no one left.

That appalling thought quickened her pace and soon the path widened out into Merlot's raised courtyard, the low sun and spreading shadows highlighting her brother drinking deep from a glass, his back to her as he glared at the elaborate water feature in the center of the patio.

Carlos. Just as she was about to call out, Alex emerged from the bar.

She shrunk back, instead taking the fork in the path that led down a gentle slope until the marble wall grew taller and taller, eventually hiding her from view. The cool stone against her shoulder goose-bumped her flesh and she suppressed a shiver.

"What the hell do you want?" she heard Carlos growl directly above her head.

"You're drunk, Carlos."

Carlos snorted. "And you're a murderous son of a bitch who's screwing my sister."

Yelena's hand went to her mouth, stifling the gasp. She glanced up but unless she took a step back, revealing her hiding place, she could see nothing but the wrought-iron railing topping the marbled wall.

"Wrong on the first one," Alex murmured, sounding way too calm. "But on the second…" The pause was long and deliberate. "What's it to you if I was?"

Something smashed close to her feet, the bitter smell of scotch assailing her nostrils a second later. "I'll kill you."

"Careful. I might think you actually mean it."

"I don't give second warnings, Alex."

Thick apprehension swirled as Yelena frowned, holding her breath.

"And I'm sure that's been enough to scare the others into silence," Alex finally said. "But it won't work with me. Not now. We both know who's been feeding those stories about my father to the press. Stories that have no basis in truth, I might add."

Carlos remained silent.

"You're itching to say it, aren't you?" Alex sounded almost amused. "So why don't I save you the trouble? You overheard a private conversation between me and my father, assumed he was cheating then used it to fuel a publicity headache, one you're hoping will sway Sprint Travel in your favor." He paused, then added almost regretfully, "Why do you hate me so much?"

Yelena could feel the heavy tension in the air. It wasn't hard to imagine Carlos's flaming glare, radiating pure fury. She'd been the recipient of that look already.

"You were the son of the great and powerful William Rush, adored by millions, the talented heir to a bloody saint." A loud crack signaled Carlos had slammed his palm on the stone wall.

"Nothing was ever handed to me on a plate. *I* had to work for it."

"So did I."

Carlos reeled off a blistering curse in Spanish, making Yelena's ears burn. "That's a crock. Nothing ever came hard to you."

"So that's what this is about—jealousy?"

"It's about getting just reward," Carlos threw back. "I've put every penny into Sprint and unlike you, I don't have an airline company and a billion-dollar resort to fall back on if it goes bust. You gave no thought to the consequences when the cops started questioning you, did you? No consideration for our partnership deal. You could've just said, 'No, I didn't do it.' Instead you hid behind a lawyer and clammed up."

"I didn't kill him, Carlos."

"I don't really care," Carlos sneered. "Our business plummeted because of you, which breaches our partnership agreement."

"And that justifies what you're doing now?"

"I'm doing what I have to to save Sprint and my reputation."

"What the hell does that mean?"

Yelena couldn't bear it any longer. She eased along the high wall until it began to dip. Just above eye level she snuck a glance over the top.

Both men were squared off, bodies rigid. Yet where the thunderous look on Carlos's face was painfully familiar, Alex seemed almost…calm. Confident, even.

"My solicitor assures me the courts will be in my favor," Carlos said now.

"Not after they know you've been slandering my family in the press." Alex placed his hands on his hips. "You'll stop this vendetta. Now."

"What vendetta?"

"Don't play dumb. We both know what you've been doing."

Carlos snorted. "Fine. But only if you hand over Sprint. And stay away from Yelena."

A raw moan of dismay rumbled in her throat but she managed to swallow it. Her hands, she noticed, clutched damp fistfuls of red satin and quickly she released her grip, furtively smoothing out the skirt.

"No."

Alex's cold response rang clearly across the courtyard, breathing life into Yelena's stiff form, warmth into her cooling limbs.

"You've got no proof," Carlos hissed. "And with a few well-chosen words in Yelena's ear, she'll drop you and your account quicker than last week's leftovers."

"She won't believe you."

"But I'm her brother. The only person she trusts. She'll believe me."

Although she couldn't read Alex's expression, his tense shoulders and angled jaw at Carlos's smug words spoke volumes.

"What Yelena and I do is none of your business, Carlos."

"Like hell it's not!" Carlos's fists tightened. "You've dragged her down to your level and I should—"

"Do not threaten me, Valero." Alex stepped into the light, his face a mask of angry impatience and dark shadow. "You can try your luck right here, right now, but I've taken on guys twice your size before and won. In fact—" his chin lifted, a tight smile stretching his lips "—go right ahead. I'm just itching to punch that pretty face of yours."

In deathly silence, Yelena watched the standoff, heart thundering, every limb and muscle alert with horrible anticipation.

Then, after interminably long seconds, Carlos slowly stepped back.

Alex shoved his hands in his pockets. "Ultimatums only work if you're holding all the cards, Carlos."

"What's that supposed to mean?"

"It means you lose. I have your threats on tape. I have proof you were talking to the press. And pretty soon I'll have proof you were stealing not only from Sprint but others, too. And more importantly, I have Yelena. Don't try it," he added tightly as Carlos rocked on his feet. "I will take you down."

Carlos's face twisted into a furious mask of rage but Alex kept going. "Keep talking to the press and you'll see how much mud sticks."

Finally Alex turned and headed across the courtyard, to the path that led back to the party. At the last minute he paused, glancing back. "You need to leave now. I'll have security drive you to the airstrip."

A stream of curses followed him as he disappeared, before Carlos turned on his heel and stalked inside.

Yelena slipped back, the lengthening shadows enveloping her. With racing heart, she placed her palms on the smooth stone, taking relief from the cold, unyielding surface against her burning skin.

This changed everything.

A few seconds passed before her body craved movement, her mind solitude. It was no surprise she ended up at the most secluded area of the resort.

The grotto was private and intimate, a small rock pool surrounded by an impressive array of trees and strategically placed slabs of granite to form a miniature version of Diamond Falls' waterfall.

She sat in a deck chair, the gentle rustle of material whispering around her legs. The bubbling, lapping water, coupled with the hypnotic ripples shimmering across the illuminated surface slowly edged into her consciousness, gently prying loose her fervent thoughts. Gradually the noise in her head eased off, leaving her with unanswered questions.

Since when had Carlos become so vindictive? How could her brother willingly set out to destroy a family? He'd never even met Pam and Chelsea.

The crystalline waters held no answer. A gentle breeze rushed through the trees, bringing with it the faraway noise of the party. Moments later, a bunch of jovial partygoers interrupted her reverie. As they laughed and joked, clumsily stripping off their formal wear, Yelena rose.

"Hey! Come and join us in the pool!"

The cute guy was grinning as he paused midstrip but Yelena shook her head with a smile. "No thanks."

Amidst their calls of disappointment, Yelena threw them an apologetic smile before clicking open the pool gate.

She kept on walking until the path stopped. Startled she glanced up, to the very last suite, which stood alone and apart from the others. Her eyes ran over the brickwork, the fancy tiled patio with its top-shelf furniture and drawn curtains.

Such perfection and beauty. Yet she wondered if the occupants would come up quite so well under scrutiny.

With a heavy sigh she turned.

"Yelena?"

She whirled, her eyes seeking the figure in the long shadows, fear pounding her heart.

A tiny click and warm light flooded the path. Alex's broad shape filled the doorway, one arm leaning against the sliding door. "Are you okay?"

Fate. She rocked on her toes, eager to leave yet unable to. Her granite resolve crumbled like dust on the wind, erased by what she'd overheard. The inexplicable urge to move surged through her then suddenly she was taking one step forward, one step, then another. "No. No, I'm not."

When he opened his arms it seemed perfectly natural to step into them. And then the tears came.

Somehow he managed to steer her inside, close the door then seat them both on his couch. And still she clung to him, savoring the feel of this huge, muscular man, taking comfort in his protective arms.

That's how he made her feel. Protected. As if he could fix anything for her.

"What happened?" he finally asked when she eventually pulled back.

Feeling a little foolish now, she dipped her head from scrutiny, quickly wiping at her cheeks. He couldn't fix this. It was something she had to get through all by herself.

"Carlos and I… we had a falling out."

"I see."

She glanced up. His expression remained neutral, waiting for her to continue.

"He…" She hesitated as everything came flooding back. "He still blames Gabriela for…well, everything. And he certainly hates me for Bella. I…I heard you both in the courtyard."

"Heard what?"

"Everything—Carlos's lies, his threats, his…"

The anguish on her face made Alex's heart ache. He reached for her hand, linking her fingers in his. "I'm sorry."

"So am I. For not seeing what he was really like sooner." When she brought those dark watery eyes up to meet his, he was a goner.

"You couldn't know," he managed to get out.

"But I should have. I should have—"

"Don't." He cupped her cheek, a sudden intimacy that shocked her into silence. This is what he had wanted, for her to see the depth of Carlos's nature, yet the victory rang hollow in the face of Yelena's pain.

Despite her tears his body reacted on an elemental level, a primitive level. Me, man. You, woman.

My woman. He'd had her once, and the urge to have her again surged through him. The guilty forbidden pleasure only heightened his need, a need far beyond his control.

A dark and terrible shard broke off inside him, disappearing into the murky waters of his past to be lost forever. In its place something sparked, something warm and hopeful.

Something that made him want things he had no right to.

She searched his face, looking for what, he didn't know. Compassion? Humanity? Whatever it was, her scrutiny undid him, unraveled the last of the control he'd been clinging onto.

When he leaned forward and kissed her, she let him, her sigh of acceptance sweet in his mouth. Her lips tasted of salt and warmth and Alex explored every inch of that flesh, from the generous swell of her bottom lip to the wide corners that would spread in mischievous abandon when she laughed.

He felt the desperate urge to hear her laugh again.

But right now, laughter was the last thing on his mind. Instead he eased her back into his soft leather couch, his hands full of her hair, his lips on her throat and his senses reeling from her sensual scent.

She shifted her weight, allowing him to settle more firmly between her legs. His manhood was already hard and throbbing and when it bumped up against her thigh, his breath rushed out on a groan.

"The floor," she got out beneath his mouth, eyes heavy with arousal.

He needed no further direction. As if she were no lighter than a doll, he scooped her up and deposited her on the carpet.

Yelena stared up at him as he made short work of his shirt, his tie already long gone. The appreciative sigh rumbled deep in her throat as he kneeled before her, purposeful intent glowing in his darkened eyes. Reaching out, she swept a hand over that broad chest, her fingers teasing from one nipple to the other.

His sharp breath made her chuckle.

Then she let her fingers trail down over his abdomen,

savoring the beautiful eroticism of those bumpy ridges, the warm yet iron-hard muscle beneath, until she got to his belt buckle.

She chanced a glance, absorbing the raw desire in his face before slowly trailing her palm down, over the large bulge of his erection.

"Lord, Yelena…" ended on a groan as she quickly unbuckled, unzipped and dragged his pants down.

He was a large man in every area. Her hand wrapped around his silken heat, quivering when he groaned again. The power she held, the power she commanded, was amazingly humble. It filled her to the brim, spilling over as she slowly bent her head.

She heard him mutter an oath as she slid him past her lips, his fingers tightening in her hair, gently urging her on. Even as the deep pulse between her legs rocketed, she took time to savor his every taste, every smell, until finally her mouth settled at the base of his groin and she murmured a satisfied sigh.

She breathed deep, filling her lungs with his pure, musky male scent, loving the way it excited her.

"Yelena…"

He was a man on the edge and losing control, his guttural command ripped from deep within. Wasting no more time, she moved, her mouth working him, loving him while his hands rested possessively on her head, guiding her pace.

It was an act so raw, so shockingly primal, loving him with her mouth. But it was also absolutely perfect. To hear his harsh breath, to feel his pounding heart, knowing she was the one giving him so much pleasure, thrilled her every single nerve.

She had the power to control a man, this man who exuded such palpable command. It numbed her thoughts. She couldn't think, she could only feel. His tight hard butt beneath her palms, the damp arousal sweating from his skin. His granite-hard erection in her mouth.

She felt his muscles quiver and in the next second, he pulled free. "Stop."

"But I haven't—"

"Sweetheart," he choked out, gently pushing her down to the floor. "I need to be inside you."

She melted right there and then, bonelessly sinking back into the plush carpet. But after he bunched her skirts around her waist, his hand searched to no avail.

Yelena grinned, twisting sideways. "Try the zipper."

They both chuckled as Alex dragged the zipper down. But amusement swiftly fled when the dress parted from her body and like Venus released from the sea, she lay bare for his inspection.

He took a deep, staggering breath. "God, you're stunning."

The raw look that passed over his face floored her, empowered her. She placed her hands behind her head, smiling, unashamedly teasing him in her black high cut G-string. "Why, thank you, kind sir."

Then he lowered his head and her smile ended as a gasp. Strong teeth teased her nipple, rolling the hard bud around his mouth, creating sudden hot friction between her legs.

He spent what felt like ages cupping the generous swell of her breasts, licking the valley between, teasing both nipples with his thumbs until she was panting, ready to explode.

"Alex, please…" She felt no shame in begging, letting him know she needed him inside her, making love to her.

And he was there, his hands spreading her thighs wide.

She held her breath, waiting, waiting. When he entered her, swift and hard, she cried out in joy.

Alex paused, heart pounding in his throat. "Did I hurt you?"

Her mouth curved into an erotic smile, her eyes fluttering

open. She could kill him with that look, all dark and wide with arousal. Then she wrapped those long legs around his waist, angling down. "No" came her breathless reply as she arched her back. "Not at all."

Her perfect neck called to him; he placed hot kisses across the length of it as she moved again, inviting him to continue.

He eagerly reared to meet her. She was so tight, so wet. He moved first in gentle strokes, then as he felt her passion begin to swiftly build, he switched to hard, almost rough thrusts. She murmured her satisfaction, meeting him all the way, tilting her hips so he could go deeper, harder.

Yelena was filled to the brim with sensory overload. He rocked her hips, grasped her bottom with skillful hands, filling her totally, completely. She felt like she could do anything, be anyone in this one moment. She was at one with him, an essential part of two halves that fit perfectly together, deep in the throes of some powerful, amazing force.

Alex's hot breath bathed her, his mouth devoured hers on the down thrust, then up again as he continued.

She was…it was…

Her eyes sprang wide, every sensitive inch of her skin throbbing, tingling with breathless climax.

She heard Alex groan as with one last thrust he emptied into her.

Oh, how she loved him.

Twelve

Yelena floated back down to earth slowly with a satisfied smile on her face, her entire body throbbing with pleasure.

With his full weight completely covering her, their flesh slick and wet, she took a deep breath. He was as necessary to her as air.

"You look pleased with yourself."

She opened her eyes into Alex's smiling ones, wicked with humor. Where their bodies joined, she could still feel him inside, intimate and hot.

She tightened her legs around him with a slow grin. "I am."

"You should be."

He rolled, taking her with him so she was on top. And when she pulled back, his hands went to her breasts, cradling the generous curves in both palms.

"You are beautiful."

She tilted her head. "So are you."

"It's official, then."

They laughed, two lovers sharing a deeply private moment. But as the seconds lengthened, Yelena's grin slowly sobered.

"Alex."

"Mmm?" He was still on her breasts, seemingly fascinated by the way her nipples pebbled beneath his thumbs.

She dragged in a sharp breath. How could she be so quickly aroused again, so soon?

"Alex. We didn't use protection."

His hands stilled, his eyes flying to hers. "Are you...?"

She felt the flush spread from belly to scalp. "I'm healthy. I've—" *Loved you for years.* She pulled in a breath before adding, "I'm fine."

"So am I."

He reached up, took her head between his hands and dragged her down for a kiss.

It wasn't a kiss full of lust and longing. It wasn't designed to arouse or command like so many others they'd shared before. Instead it was tender, soft. Loving. Yet more than the others, it made Yelena's blood pump faster, her lungs swell, her heart sing.

She let herself get swept away on the moment, let her mind take her to a place where she and Alex were together, where Bella completed their perfect family and they all lived happily ever after.

Yet she could only indulge in the fantasy for so long because slowly, her head began to fill with questions and doubts, ones that became too loud to ignore.

"Alex?"

"Mmm?" He'd moved down to her throat, his hands still holding her in place. She groaned as her body responded with sluggish delight.

She wanted to tell him her deepest secrets right then, let him know exactly how she felt. Yet fear robbed her of courage.

Alex put a high price on the truth. Would he want her after he knew she'd been lying all along?

"Was Carlos right? Did you hire me to get back at him?"

Her questions had the desired effect: his questing hands stilled, his head angling back to take her in.

"Do you really want me to answer that?"

Abruptly she withdrew, backing up against the couch, pillow clutched to her chest. "Which means yes."

Alex's thoughts tangled at the look on her face. "You know Bennett & Harper are the best in the business. That you are exceptional at what you do." He held up a hand at her impatient frown. "And yes, I did start out angry and desperate to cause Carlos damage. But then—"

"Then, what?"

"I didn't want to anymore."

Her brow wrinkled. "You didn't want to sleep with me?"

Lord, she undid him. "I didn't want Carlos to be the reason," he explained, taking her hand. When he brought it to his lips, her eyes widened. "There's never been a moment I've not wanted to make love to you, Yelena."

He watched her face relax, her eyes go liquid. Then she blinked and shook herself.

"You used me," she said flatly.

Her eyes, so dark and expressive, wounded him to the core. He could dredge up excuses but shame humbled him. He nodded. "I know. And I'm sorry."

She studied him for another moment before her chin tipped up. "Why did you invite Carlos tonight?"

"Because I needed you to see him for who he really is."

"You couldn't just tell me?" But even as the words left her mouth Yelena realized how stupid she sounded. She wouldn't have believed him. Not then. But now…

"And he's been going to the papers."

His chest tightened but he forced himself to relax. "Yes."

Yelena stared past his shoulder to the opposite wall in silence.

"I'll get my proof. About everything."

The silence stretched again until Alex said gently, "Look, Yelena, I know he's your brother but—"

"You've got to understand something about Carlos," she said firmly, bring her eyes back to his. "His reputation, his… his…" She struggled for the words, hand accentuating her dilemma. "His obsession with being who he is and what that stands for is the only thing he cares about. You know what it was like at school—no one touched the Valero girls. It was flattering having an overprotective brother. Gabriela hated it but had no choice, given what had happened back home. And when I got older, it became…"

"Stifling."

She nodded. "It was never about me. It was about him and his perfect reputation."

"Yelena…"

"He's never held Bella, not once." Her breath caught, a dead giveaway to her distress. "He never even asks about her."

She finally sees how Carlos really is. Alex wanted to pump his fist in the air, shout out his victory, but triumph was tempered by the obvious pain that shone in her eyes.

Then Yelena said, "So what Carlos heard…what I heard. Your father *wasn't* having an affair?"

His heart paused. "No."

"Then what were you arguing about?"

"Nothing important."

He rose in one fluid movement, so abrupt Yelena involuntarily gasped.

"Alex…?"

"I'm telling you to leave it, Yelena."

She paused. It was his voice, all rawness and jagged angles, a stark contrast to the smooth way he pulled on his pants.

He was damaged. Oh, not on the outside, because Alex

Rush had perfected a polished façade of control and restraint as necessary to his survival as breathing. No, it was something deeper, something missing.

She knew him. *Really* knew him, and not in the casual-date way Gabriela had cheerfully described before Yelena had cut her off, red-faced. And not in the "my business partner, Alex Rush" Carlos had bragged about.

Was she the only one who could see into his heart, see the cloying demons that touched his soul, ones she knew came from his picture-perfect home, ones he refused to address?

"I won't leave it," she said firmly. "Please tell me, Alex."

He rounded on her so suddenly, with such fury blazing from his eyes that she jumped.

"I said, leave it! Just because we had sex does not give you carte blanche to my entire life!"

She felt the slap as surely as palm meeting skin. Blood fled from her face, the dark truth a hard lump in her chest.

"So I'm just good enough to sleep with, is that it?"

Disgust hit Alex's stomach the exact moment shock distorted her features. He took one step back, dropped his eyes to the floor with a growl. It was done. He couldn't undo it now. *Way to go, mate.* The slow, victory clap of his conscience rang hollow in his ears. *You've been looking for a way to push her away and now you've found it.*

"I think I should go." She reached for her dress, a flush staining those high cheekbones.

He groaned. "Yelena, you don't have to—"

She shot him a look as she fumbled with her clothing, finally dragging the dress over those beautiful curves. "I'm flying home tomorrow, remember? I need to focus on your campaign."

Yelena grabbed her shoes then hurried to the door, silence dogging her retreat. Yet as she cracked the door open, she forced herself to glance back.

Alex had picked up the remote control and was flicking

through the channels, his bare back so painfully straight that her hands ached to touch him, to help ease the tension bunched along those beautiful shoulders.

Her throat tightened, choking whatever breath she had left.

"You need to think about this situation with Carlos and Sprint Travel. If you fight him for it, it'll hit the papers. It could turn ugly and overshadow what we're trying to achieve here."

The efficiently spare nod, along with a gruff "I will" was her only acknowledgment.

Pain sliced her heart but she managed to hold it together until she walked out, closing the door behind with an inaudible click.

Yelena paused in the corridor, the subdued lights throwing her shadow across the pristine white walls. Gently she placed a hand on the door.

"I love you."

She wanted to shout it loud instead of whispering into the empty silence. She loved Alex Rush.

Slowly she dragged herself down the hall, muscles aching with delicious exertion, shoes dangling from her fingers, the hem of her dress bunched in her hand.

She understood Alex better than he thought she did. He was an exceedingly proud man, one who did not take attacks on his family lying down.

She finally made it to her door and fumbled in her purse for the keycard. A wave of guilt lapped at her heels as she softly made her way inside. Alex wouldn't lie about Carlos. Not about something this important. And she'd heard it with her own ears. Her brother was behind those awful rumors, not only trying to destroy Alex's reputation, but also Pam's and Chelsea's in the process. Three innocent people.

And then there was her own bombshell. How would Alex take that?

She gently woke Jasmine, who'd fallen asleep on her couch, then took a quick shower. As the smell of Alex washed from her body, her mind went into overdrive, senses inundated as she recalled every second, every passionate moment of their lovemaking.

She loved him.

For another hour she lay awake in her enormous bed, the feather quilt bunched about her waist as she tossed and turned.

A tiny cry permeated the silence and Yelena rose with relief, padded into Bella's room and scooped her up in her arms.

In the semidarkness she gently jogged the hungry baby, cooing softly as she took the bottle from the fridge, heated it then settled on the sofa.

"Is it wrong that I don't want to tell him, Bella?" she whispered softly as the baby fed. "I promised Gabriela I'd keep our secret and keep you safe…" She trailed off, her fingers tightening around the bottle. She recalled Alex's fury, his pain, when he'd first seen Bella on the plane.

"He still thinks you're mine." And as much as she desperately wished Bella was hers in every sense, she knew the lie would eventually come between them. Not right now, not in the first flush of desire and lust. No, it'd be later, when the bonds of trust were again strong between them.

That is, if there *was* a later. Alex was desperate to push her away. And right now, she had the awful feeling it would be easier—and safer—if she let him.

After her restless night, Yelena was determined to focus on work the next morning before the midday flight took her back to reality. But instead of going to her makeshift office where the chance of running into Alex was high, she made a detour for Ruby's.

Breakfast and coffee, she reasoned. Plus the added bonus of people watching in case her thoughts wandered.

She needn't have worried—when she clicked on to the morning's papers to check last night's coverage, one small article caught her eye. Quickly she read, a deep frown forming. According to the reporter's skillful prose that skirted the edges of truth, she and Alex were deep in the throes of a secret affair.

"Yelena, do you have a minute?"

Yelena blinked up from her laptop screen to Pamela Rush, who stood next to her booth, eyes hidden behind large sunglasses. Her fingers played with the plaited belt at her waist, telling Yelena something was off.

With a reassuring smile, she clicked the laptop closed.

"Sure. Take a seat." She nodded to the vacant spot opposite, then gestured to a waiter. "Would you like a drink?"

"Iced tea, please," Pam said automatically, giving the waiter a smile as she removed her glasses.

Yelena waited patiently as Pam carefully folded her sunglasses on the table, then recentered the coaster. Finally, the older woman linked her fingers and glanced out to the entertainment area, to the view of the semicrowded pool beyond.

"A lovely day for a swim."

"Mmm. Did you stay long last night?"

Pam smiled. "About ten. The bands were still going when I left. And Chelsea looked to be having a good time."

Yelena nodded, smiling back.

A brief pause, then Pam said, "You're leaving today."

"Yes." Yelena nodded. "Now that we've started the ball rolling I need to get a team together, start organizing details for the anniversary, plus put a few feelers out for some one-on-one interviews."

Pam looked surprised. "Alex has agreed to it?"

"Last night was a start. I'm working on it," Yelena added with a rueful smile.

"Ah." Pam paused, her fingers going to a thin, elegant diamond ring on her left hand, methodically turning it around and around. "Chelsea and you have been getting along well."

"She's a great kid."

Pam nodded. "Thank you. She's been so angry for so long—I suggested therapy but she balked at that. Which would be fine except she wasn't talking to anyone, me and Alex included. I'm grateful she's had someone to open up to. Which is what brings me here." She petered off and took a breath. "I need you to organize an interview."

Yelena eased back in her seat. "For you?"

Pam nodded, her gaze direct. Those dark blue depths contained a multitude of feelings—pride, honesty. And fear.

"Does Alex know?"

"No. He'd just try and talk me out of it." Her face turned stormy. "I love him, Yelena, but he always takes on too much responsibility for this family. He's always has been my little protector, ever since he was a boy." Her smile was bittersweet, speaking of pain long buried. "No, this is for me, Yelena. I need to do this."

Impulsively Yelena reached across the table and placed her hand on Pam's, looking her straight in the eye. "Okay."

Pam nodded, her relieved sigh coming out in a rush. "Thank you."

Yelena withdrew to make a note in her diary. "And the other thing?"

At the sudden silence Yelena glanced up. Pam's fingers were linked together on the table top.

"How is your gorgeous baby?"

Yelena smiled. "Sleeping at the moment. Pam…"

"Yelena." Pam's hand shot out to cover Yelena's, her fingers suddenly cold despite the warmth of the morning. "I'm sorry. I need to ask you something."

"Yes?"

"It's a personal question. I'm sorry," she repeated and quickly pulled her hand back. "But it's been eating at me ever since you arrived and, well…"

"Pam," Yelena said slowly. "Whatever it is, I'll try my best to answer it."

Her face flushing, Pam said, "I have to know. Is your… I mean…" Her gaze dropped to the table as she finally whispered, "Before all this. Did you and Alex…were you…?"

Yelena sat back in her chair. "Did Alex and I ever date?"

"Sort of." Pam's face flushed deeper. "Were you and he ever…intimate?"

With a tangled tongue, Yelena stared at the deeply mortified woman. The silence lasted until the waiter brought their drinks and moved on to the next table.

"No," Yelena finally managed as she grabbed the cold, tall glass. "Can I ask why you want to know?"

The woman's shoulders sagged. "Thank you for being honest. It's obviously just my eyes playing tricks. Ever since I saw that sweet little baby of yours, well…" She gave a little laugh, wavy with embarrassment. "Bella is the spitting image of Alex and Chelsea at that age—same nose, same chin. And you and Alex do have some chemistry—" She quickly cut herself off with a faltering smile. "Put it down to my eagerness at wanting to be a grandma. Well…" She rose from her seat, palming her glass. "I should let you get back to work. Thank you."

Yelena watched Pam go, her brow furrowed. Odd. Very odd. As if Bella would be—

A terrible, ridiculous thought crashed in, leaving her gasping as the world suddenly tilted on its access. Everything—her brain, her breath, her very heartbeat—came to a screeching sickening halt.

Oh, no. Oh, no, no, no. Gabriela hadn't… She would have told her.

There was no way on earth her baby sister had lain in that small hospital, bleeding to death after she'd given birth, using the last breath in her body to *lie* to her. Which could only mean one possible thing—Gabriela hadn't known who Bella's father was.

With jerky movements, she flipped open her diary, back to last year's calendar. Her finger shakily traced the dates, skipping backwards as she counted.

Alex and Gabriela had been dating on and off since May. She paused on July then tapped her finger thoughtfully. Too many things had happened that month—Gabriela returning from Madrid, the embassy ball. Alex kissing her.

Her heart bottomed out, leaving a terrible numbness in its wake.

What was she supposed to do now?

Thirteen

Emotionally exhausted, Yelena was unfazed when her family's official chauffeur greeted her arrival at Canberra airport. She got into her father's car and strapped Bella in, resigned silence accompanying the drive to the Valero residence.

The car drove along Morshead Drive, then left onto the King's Avenue Bridge that took her over Lake Burley Griffin. As they headed towards Capital Hill and Parliament House, Yelena watched the steady flow of traffic. Soon the change of landscape told her they were in Yarralumla. The affluent suburb was populated by foreign diplomats, politicians and various families of Canberra's super rich, and it showed— from the neat gardens, the subtle and not-so-subtle homes, even the streets themselves. Meticulous and groomed, that's what the area reflected.

When the car drew to a halt in the long curving driveway, Yelena finally broke from her apathy. A Valero summons meant only one thing—displeasure.

She got out of the car, shouldering Bella as she studied what had had once been her home. She still loved the look of those white rendered walls, terra-cotta tiles and clean, smooth angles that made up the seven-bedroomed, two-storied house. And as always, the gardens were superbly groomed, the windows sparkling.

But it had always been her parents' house, never hers. This thought was confirmed when she stepped into the living area, an aura of "look, don't touch" permeating every square inch from its high ceiling to its timber floor and period features.

On the beautiful antique couch sat her perfectly groomed mother, legs crossed elegantly at the ankles, skirt demurely covering her knees. Her father stood behind, dark and towering, a scowl on his autocratic face. To the left, Carlos leaned against the polished bar, a glass of amber liquid cradled in his hand.

"What is this, an intervention?" Yelena joked lamely, even as her grip tightened on Bella.

A servant came forward, hovering expectantly. Yelena frowned.

"Let Julie settle the baby," Juan commanded.

Yelena blinked. "Why?"

"Because we need to talk."

"So talk." Yelena glared at the unfortunate Julie, who had flushed deep red.

"*Dios.*" Juan sighed and waved the servant away. "Fine. I don't need to remind you, Yelena, that I am not happy with your continued association with Alexander Rush."

Her eyes flicked to Carlos. He met her gaze head-on as he slowly took a sip from his glass.

"It not only impacts on you," Juan continued sternly. "It affects everyone in this family."

"How?"

"People talk, Yelena," Maria said tightly. "Your father—

this family—has a reputation to uphold in this community. Rumors and malicious gossip can damage it irreparably."

"The same way the ones circulating about William Rush's affair are destroying his family?"

It wasn't her mother's reaction she was after, although Maria's moue of distaste was satisfying. No, she carefully watched Carlos' eyes narrow, a second before his expression smoothed out.

"Yes," Juan said. "The longer you continue associating with the Rushes, the more damage it will cause."

Yelena sighed, her hand automatically going to Bella's back as she felt the baby stir. She was tired, so very tired of these mind games. The burden of respectability and family honor weighed heavily on her shoulders, dragging her down, warring with her own sense of right.

"I'm sorry if you feel that way, Papá. But Bennett & Harper signed a contract—"

"Then get out of it. No one's indispensible—surely you can hand the job over to someone else?"

His unconscious insult slapped her firmly in the face and she felt her cheeks color. "No, Papá. Even if I wanted out— which I don't—I have a promotion riding on this."

Juan's eyes narrowed. "I did not *ask* you to withdraw, Yelena."

Chagrin welled up, chasing away her fatigue. "So your wishes are more important than my career, my life?"

"We are talking about the Valero name," Carlos said curtly. "About our public reputation, our—"

"Oh, how I am sick to death of hearing that!" she hissed. "Especially from you, someone who claims diplomatic immunity every time he gets a speeding ticket."

"Yelena," Juan rumbled ominously.

"You held the 'reputation' card over Gabriela's head for years and where did that get her?"

"Yelena!" Maria and Juan echoed in unison.

"She's dead. And still you're so ashamed of her you refuse to let people know. Despite everything she did, despite how disappointed you were, I *loved* her." Her voice cracked then, a sob tearing at her throat. Bella let out a grumble, sensitive to her mother's distress and Yelena immediately started rubbing her back.

"Of course you did. We all did," Carlos said quickly.

Surprised, Yelena stared at him, until Maria added, "But she was also uncontrollable and selfish." Her mother's mouth thinned, a red-lipsticked slash of displeasure. "Even when we moved here, she was still the same reckless girl. I *know* you saw that."

"When she was *sixteen*," Yelena said, exasperated. "So she dropped out of school, modeled for a few chain-store catalogs. But she quit modeling, she had a regular job. She wanted to move on from her past but you all just wouldn't let her."

"That is enough, Yelena!" Juan thundered, making everyone jump. A second later, Bella let out a mighty wail.

Yes, it was enough. Yelena shifted Bella to her other shoulder, patting her firmly through the warm layers. "It suited you all to keep her tied to her past mistakes, to use her as an example. But she deserved better. She was my *sister.* And if this is the way you treat people in this family, then I don't want to be a part of it anymore."

Every face in the room displayed their own version of total and utter shock and for long seconds, triumph spiked Yelena's blood. A short-lived triumph when mortification quickly flushed her burning cheeks.

She turned on her heel, stalked out the living room and down the hallway, her clipped footsteps echoing on the polished slate.

With a hefty wrench she pulled the front door open and the blast of cold air hit her hot face.

What have you done?

Panic crept in, spreading its insidious tentacles of doubt

and uncertainty, but for the first time she kept right on going, down the steps and across the driveway, to the car that still waited.

You've done it. You're free. Instead of the crushing sense of loss she'd expected from this moment, relief mingling with tentative joy lifted her heart.

She patted Bella, warm and comforting against her chest. She was well and truly alone now. Yes, there was fear of the unknown, but she'd overcome that before. She'd do it again.

"Yelena!"

She whipped her head around to see Carlos slowly jogging to catch up to her. When he stopped, his small smile oozed nervous contrition. "Look, I think I owe you an apology."

Her heart gave a small cautious jump. "For what?"

"For what happened on Saturday night. I'd had a few drinks and things just got a little...heated."

Yelena let the silence flow around them. Despite the half-hearted apology, the pain of his rejection still throbbed under the surface.

"So I'm sorry, okay? Okay?"

His smile spread wider, one eyebrow curving up as he tilted his head in that charismatic way she'd seen a thousand times before. But now, after everything she'd seen and heard, she was immune. Instead of giving him an answering smile, she forced her expression to remain impassive.

"Here, let me get this." He opened the car door and stepped aside.

What does he want? The thought lingered as she bent to strap Bella in the baby capsule.

"So...you're still seeing him?"

Her body stiffened but she kept on with her task. "He's my client."

When she straightened, Carlos had shoved his hands in his pockets, staring down at his feet.

A perfect picture of reluctant gossip. *Oh, come on.* It was all Yelena could do not to roll her eyes. Instead she scowled, which only seemed to appease Carlos.

"Then you should know he called this morning and threatened me."

Threatened? That wasn't Alex's style but she was way too tired to tell Carlos that. "And why are you telling me this?"

"Because I need your help."

She slowly leaned against the doorframe. "How?"

He paused for effect. If she didn't know any better she'd peg him as reluctant, even embarrassed. But she did know him, all too well.

"I was thinking—and I know this is a lot to ask, and I wouldn't normally do this—"

"Carlos…"

His irritation showed in the brief downward turn of his mouth. "If you could have a word with him, maybe convince him not to—"

The sharp inward sound of Yelena's horrified breath silenced him.

"No."

Carlos's expression tightened. "So you'd let this stupid vendetta go to court? How is this going to impact on us? Our parents? Your campaign?" He added in a moment of inspiration.

With cool deliberation, she got in the car, slid down the window then closed the door with a firm clunk.

"Carlos," she said slowly as she slid her sunglasses into place. "Let me say this once and once only. I heard you and Alex by the pool on Saturday night. As much as you're my brother and I love you, I will not—cannot—trust you. You've hurt too many people, including me, for us to ever be okay again."

As she turned to clip herself in, Carlos slapped a hand on the window frame, making her jump.

"So you're choosing *him* over your own family?"

She sighed. Surely her heart couldn't break anymore, not when she knew the full extent of Carlos's malice? Yet a tiny piece still cracked, reminding her of the brother she'd once blindly adored.

"Yes, I am."

His stunned expression gave her no satisfaction as she powered up the window. As the car drove away for the very last time, she knew where she had to be—with people who needed her love and support, who'd been damaged terribly by the actions of someone she'd loved. She needed to help make amends.

And slowly, the pain in her heart began to retreat.

Fourteen

It was Tuesday. Yelena had been gone nearly two days. Two long, arduous, maddening days, days full of work, of papers and files and copious amounts of coffee.

Days without Yelena.

Despite the constant influx of people and the work load, Diamond Bay seemed empty somehow. With his mother and Chelsea on a shopping trip in Sydney and Yelena gone, the gaping hole was even more obvious.

It was so not like him to be this unfocused, this distracted. A handful of times he'd glanced up at his office door, certain Yelena was about to walk in with that mesmerizing hip sway that sucked him in every time.

But she wouldn't. He'd seen to that.

So he'd punished himself by playing every encounter over in his head until, as the early morning sun began to blaze over the horizon, he'd jumped on his bike and zoomed off.

Now he'd been on the road for an hour but still the grueling heat couldn't wipe Yelena from his mind.

He drove, mile after mile of red dust, the hard, throbbing machine between his thighs and the gutsy roar of the engine in his ears as he burned up the road, on his way somewhere, anywhere that didn't have a memory of her, her mouth and that hot lush skin he'd possessed so completely.

With the sun blazing high in the sky, he finally paused for a breather. The desert heat hit him full force as he yanked off his helmet, tarmac hot beneath his boots, searing up through his leathers as he swiped the beaded sweat from his forehead.

No matter how far he rode he couldn't outrun *her*. Their last night together spun dizzyingly in his head, forcing him to focus on the one thing he wanted to forget.

With a curse he hurled his helmet, scowling as it hit the ground in a shower of red dust.

And in that moment, something deep and yearning inside him cracked wide open. It made him want things, things that only Yelena could give him.

He recalled the feel of the hot, sweet body beneath his, how she'd welcomed him inside with almost frantic desire in her dark eyes. She'd tasted like always—sexy skin, want barely restrained. She'd looked amazing, from the wild cloud of hair spilling over lush breasts, to the way her waist indented and flared into sinfully curvy hips.

His groin tightened painfully with the memories. Of dipping his tongue into her belly button before dragging his mouth across that perfect belly, the skin hot and reactive to his touch...

A perfect belly.

He paused with a frown. Perfect belly, perfect hips, perfect breasts.

He snapped in a sharp breath, mind racing backwards. He hadn't just been swept up in the moment. Her skin *was* perfect.

No stretch marks, no C-section scar.

Realization instantaneously heated into rage, and rage into

fiery knives of pain, tiny pinpricks stabbing into every muscle, every nerve.

She'd lied to him.

He was on the bike in less than a second, racing back to Diamond Bay, to Yelena.

To the truth.

He stormed into the resort like the hounds of hell themselves were snapping at his heels, uncaring of the stares, the whispers left in his wake. His jerking strides devoured the long hallway and when he slapped his hand on Yelena's office door, it crashed back on its hinges with a satisfying crack.

Nostrils flared, blood thumping, he took in the empty room at first with fury, then dawning realization.

She's gone, you fool.

He gave a groan before viciously unzipping his jacket and pulling out his phone. He palmed it, poised to dial, but an e-mail reminder flashed on the screen and his whole body stilled.

Re: Pamela Rush interview

All his veins felt as if they'd suddenly frozen, leaving him unable to even breathe. Then panic quickly rushed in, forcing his heart rate up, tightening his lungs. With a few taps he was reading an e-mail from a Leah Jackson at Bennett & Harper.

It was confidential, obviously sent to him by mistake. As fury mounted, he scanned down, finally getting to the original exchange between Yelena and the show's producer.

Thanks for fitting us in on Tuesday, Rita, Yelena had written. *My client is anxious for the public to hear her story and I'm sure you'll agree it's a powerful one. I appreciate you giving us approval over final cut and I'm positive there will be no major problems with this.*

He slumped in the chair, his pounding heartbeat a deep echo in his brain. Then in the next second, he dialed the office phone.

"It's Alex Rush. Organize a car and have the airstrip fire up my plane. I'll be leaving for Canberra in twenty minutes."

Yelena stood behind the lighting stand, watching the makeup girl dust Pam's face with powder. "Are you sure you want me here?" she asked for the third time.

Pam smiled. "You've made all this possible, Yelena. Why wouldn't I want you here?"

Chelsea stood beside Yelena, giving her hand a reassuring squeeze. She'd taken her suggestion and talked to her mother all right, and it had resulted in a full-blown report for *Morning Grace,* Australia's most-watched current affairs/breakfast show. So here they were, in Pam's sun room in the Canberra "mausoleum" house. Masses of afternoon light streamed through the glass walls, falling squarely on Pam, seated alone on the comfortable couch.

Guilt swept Yelena's conscience. Alex was her client, he was the one who'd signed the contract, the one who was paying Bennett & Harper. No matter how much she knew Pam needed to do this, Alex would accuse her of going behind his back. And he'd be right. Yet she was human. Pam had a right to let the public know the real truth, even if it did mean losing Alex's trust in the process. At least he'd be cleared once and for all for his father's death.

Admit it. You're afraid. Afraid that you'll reveal everything to him with one look from those all-seeing blue eyes.

And that would mean losing control of everything she'd worked so hard for since Gabriela died.

She glanced at Pam, who was studying her with disturbing thoroughness. "We couldn't wait," Yelena added. "It was either now if we wanted to make tomorrow's show, or wait another two months."

"I know. It's time," Pam said softly, her troubled blue eyes stormy as the makeup girl finally finished. "I need to speak out, especially with that thing in today's paper."

Yelena flushed, knowing Carlos was probably behind the two-part article scheduled to hit Sydney's *Daily Mirror* come Monday. She'd got a heads-up barely twenty-four hours before, the promo ad screaming from the front page with voyeuristic glee.

"I need to let people know the truth," Pam said softly, her eyes going to Chelsea. Suddenly her face, so elegant and refined, crumpled. "I love you, sweetheart."

"I love you too, Mum," Chelsea choked out. Her fingers tightened around Yelena's and Yelena squeezed back.

Here were two amazing women, facing their demons and speaking out to the world. Their strength and courage floored Yelena, her throat tight as she choked back tears.

Her head was one big mess, what with Alex, Carlos, the upcoming exposé and now Pam's interview. And sitting back in her little apartment, burning a hole in her briefcase, lay the means to possibly shatter her future: forms for the DNA test that would prove or disprove this ridiculous suspicion regarding Bella's paternity.

If Alex wasn't the father then what would be the point of revealing she'd lied before the results proved it either way? Yet short of stealing his hair or bodily fluids, how could she get a DNA sample *without* telling him?

She'd wrestled with her conscience at Diamond Bay until her call to Channel Five had provided a convenient escape. But now, with everything crowding in on her, she couldn't stop her mind from going there.

You love him. He needs to be told.

She glanced up as Grace Callahan settled in the chair opposite Pam, fixed on a mike then nodded to the segment producer.

The producer called for quiet, said, "And…go!" and they were off.

"Pamela Rush, can you start from the beginning and tell us

why you decided to do this interview after all these months of silence?"

When Yelena felt Chelsea's fingers tighten in hers, she gave the teenager a reassuring smile. An awful sadness weighted her heart, creating a pall over what should have been a triumphant moment for her career, for Pam and Chelsea and the truth.

If these two women could take control and put things right, why couldn't she?

It was close to five o'clock before the crew packed up.

"What's going to happen to Mum now?"

Chelsea had been picking at her fingernails for the last ten minutes, her face fraught with concern. "Will she go to jail?"

Yelena met Pam's look. The older woman nodded.

"We don't know. George says it depends on what the police want to do," Yelena said, deferring the situation to their newly hired criminal lawyer. "Your mother did provide a false statement."

"But there are also mitigating circumstances," Pam added as Chelsea's expression turned fearful. "I've arranged to go into the station and make a formal statement tomorrow morning."

"But she could be arrested," Chelsea said.

Pam nodded slowly. "It's possible, yes."

Chelsea clutched her mother's hand, her fingers firm as her chin went up.

"Don't worry, Chelsea." Yelena smiled bravely even as her heart constricted. "We'll work this out. And George is one of the best. We're going to try our hardest to ensure your mother doesn't spend any time in jail. I'll be there for you both."

After a few tear-ridden hugs, Yelena finally left, giving both Pam's and Chelsea's hands another reassuring squeeze and murmuring positive reassurances.

It took twenty minutes to drive out of affluent Yarralumla

until finally hitting the Commonwealth Bridge, another five until she wound her way around Canberra's multiple roundabouts before turning the corner to her city apartment complex.

She was going to do her damnedest to ensure the Rushes were not punished further, which meant putting a stop to those slanderous articles. And *that* meant dealing with Carlos.

A dark blue Mercedes sat directly in front of her building, a familiar figure standing ramrod straight by the passenger door. Her breath sped out. Even at this distance, she could see Alex's tension bristle from every muscle in his broad, commanding body.

She pulled into the basement car park, heart in her throat, dread freezing her fingers as she took the key from the ignition. When she got out and turned, he was right there, hands on his hips, face tight with barely leashed emotion.

"Alex! What—what are you doing here?" She readjusted the bundle of files she held, a poor barrier of protection.

With a dark scowl he shoved his phone under her nose. Blinking, she took a step back, but not before she recognized the e-mail on the screen.

Her heart bottomed out and she winced.

With a furious question in his eyes, he yanked his phone back. "Get in the car, Yelena."

"Why?"

"Would you prefer we do this out in the open?" His voice bounced off the cement pylons, echoing in the cavernous silence as his eyes skimmed the car park. "Or upstairs in front of your *daughter?*"

Yelena's stomach clenched. She nodded, swinging open the door of her shiny BMW then closing it firmly.

After he got in the passenger side she expected unleashed fury, a blast of accusations and demands. After the crazy day she'd had, she was fully prepared to accept whatever he threw at her. Yet he just glared at her, blue eyes slowly picking her apart with ruthless efficiency.

She fidgeted, first with her necklace, then with the edges of the files she still clutched.

"You went ahead with an interview after I'd specifically told you not to." He finally got out. "Why?"

"Because it was Pam's choice, Alex."

"This is *not* what I hired you for."

"But it's what she wanted."

She could see his jaw working as he fought to bring his emotions under control. His eyes, now flashing with bitterness, held something else, something odd and infinitely more scary. "So instead of letting me know, I have to find out via e-mail?"

"That was a mistake—"

"Oh, and that makes it all better." His face contorted into harsh planes, freezing her out. "Do not presume" came his tight reply, "to know anything about what's happened in my life, Yelena."

"How can I, when you don't tell me?" She took a deep breath. *He's vulnerable and angry, lashing out.* "I was there at Pam's interview. I know your father controlled every aspect of your family's lives. I know he hit Pam regularly. I know he hit you until *you* were old enough to fight back." She paused, remembering Pam's stiff, heartrending recollection. "You never left home because you were scared he'd start on Chelsea—"

"Stop."

She ignored the dangerous warning. "That night in your office. You were talking about your father leaving your *mother* alone, weren't you?"

"I said, stop!"

His deafening command made her flinch, the venom washing over her like some horrid stain. With eyes wide and muscles taut, she stared, until the furious lines on his face suddenly melted into anguish, then horror.

"Yelena, I…" He lifted a hand then quickly dropped it, revulsion reflected in his eyes. "I didn't mean to… I'd never lay a finger on you, you know that."

She took a breath, then another, her whole body humming. "I know."

"He never touched Chelsea," he choked out, his face contorted. "She adored him. And I covered for that bastard because I didn't want to shatter her illusions."

Just like yours were. She could have wept then but one look at his face, his strong, implacable face tinged with self-disgust and she dared not.

"Chelsea knew, Alex. She'd seen it happen a month before his death," she said softly. Shock stiffened his body, just before the pain poured in, pain that wrenched at her own heart.

"That night we were together…when I came home…" He dragged a hand over his face, raw emotion carved into every line, every muscle.

"Tell me, Alex. Tell me what happened."

"I don't know!" He banged his fists softly on the dashboard. "I came home and he was in the pool. And Mum…"

"She didn't fall asleep watching television like she told the police."

Still he said nothing, just stared out the window, a faraway look on his face. Yelena placed a tentative hand on his leg, a gesture aimed at soothing, consoling. Yet it was like touching fire-forged steel.

"Alex. You're not alone in this. I want to be here for you."

His head snapped up so quickly she jumped.

"How can you when you lied to me?" His jaw tightened, eyes narrowing. "When you *still* lie."

"I…"

"You let me believe Bella was yours."

She faced his disappointment, small and still with the burden of guilt he'd unexpectedly laid on her. "How did you know?"

"No scars or stretch marks."

"I see." She sighed.

"Is that all you have to say?"

She shot him a fierce look. "She *is* mine, Alex, in all the ways that count. My name is on her birth certificate. I raised her, I love her."

"But you are not her natural mother."

Her heart ripped from her chest, sending a screaming ache into her brain. "No."

"Whose is she?" He paused, considering her as a beat passed. Then his face contorted with realization. "Gabriela's."

"Yes." One word yet she could barely get it out.

"So why didn't you tell me?"

She felt sudden tears well in her eyes before she quickly blinked them away. "Because Gabriela made me promise before she died. That night I left you, the night your father died…" When she dragged her eyes up to his, his frozen look broke her heart a little more. "Gabriela was involved with Salvatore Vitto."

He frowned. "The Spanish drug lord?"

She nodded. "Gabriela had no idea—they'd been on and off since they'd met a few years back, at some agency party in Madrid." She couldn't meet his eyes, knowing her distaste for Gabriella's multi-boyfriend habit was not the issue right now. "When she returned in June she found out and broke it off, which was when he abducted her. She…" She swallowed. "She called me on the run and I met her at the airport. To make sure we weren't followed, we crisscrossed Europe for weeks. Then we ended up in Germany."

The horror of those few months flooded back, sending her hands trembling. She clasped her fingers firmly together and placed them in her lap.

"Bella was born on the eighteenth of March, one week before her due date, in a small German hospital with Gabriela registered as me. In order for the dates to fit my pregnancy, I had to claim she was two months premature when I applied for her passport. You can't fly with premie babies so I had to wait until May to return home." She took a breath then continued, "Vitto is a vicious, ruthless man. Gabriela had no doubt he'd kill her and take Bella if he ever found out."

A small, strangled sound. When she looked up, she thought she saw something more on his face, a small crack in that perfect shield of composure he showed to the world.

"Why didn't you come home before Bella was born?"

"Vitto had Gabriela's passport. We couldn't risk getting a new one in Spain, not when he had government officials in his pocket. When we finally got to the Australian embassy in Germany, we'd been anonymous and trouble free for a month. By that time Gabriela was showing and didn't want to come home. I tried talking her around but you know how stubborn she could be."

Despite the gravity of the moment, he gave a brief, spare smile and a curt nod.

"And you could imagine my parents' reaction if she came back pregnant and unwed." Well-worn frustration sparked, stiffening her posture. "My father and Carlos, demanding to know who the father was, horrified the Valero name was again tarnished. My mother, mortified and disgraced in front of all her social peers. My God—all the questions, the accusations, the yelling, on and on and on." She tightened her grip on the files and pain sliced her fingers. "Of course, I was the shining example of all things good and proper. I cannot remember one single lecture to Gabriela when her exploits weren't followed with 'why can't you be more like your sister?' She made out like it didn't matter, but the comparison killed me every time."

She stared out the windscreen, too afraid to meet his eyes, to see that familiar icy shield shutting her out.

"And yet you willingly posed as an unwed single mother."

"I had to protect Bella. A blemish on my sterling reputation was a small price to pay for her life."

This was it. This was the moment. She took a deep cleansing breath. She was afraid, of course—willingly sacrificing control went against everything she'd struggled for since Gabriela had died. She'd had to be strong, strong for Bella, strong for her dead sister.

Yet as she finally looked up into Alex's eyes, that strength began to bend like a tree caught in a hurricane.

"Alex? I need to tell you something else."

A dry laugh, full of tight irony, emerged from his lips. "Oh, please. Be my guest."

"Upstairs."

He glanced towards the elevator bank, then back to her. Yelena nodded. It was time for her, too.

Fifteen

In her living room, amongst the well-loved collection of books, antiques and modern comfy furniture, he paced. He reminded Yelena of Canberra Zoo's tigers—majestic, proud yet ultimately aggravated with containment.

She approached him slowly. "Did you and Gabriela ever sleep together?"

He stopped dead in his tracks. "What kind of question is—"

"Please, Alex. I need to know."

His frown became darker. "Once. At the Christmas in July ball. It was after our kiss. You'd shot me down, I got drunk and she was there..."

She knew the moment he trailed off. He paled.

"You think Bella is mine?"

"I assumed Vito was the father. And from her actions, so did Gabriela. She never even mentioned you and her..." Yelena felt her cheeks warm as she broke off. "But the dates fit. And your mother mentioned a resemblance to you and Chelsea when you were babies."

He stepped back so quickly it left Yelena breathless. Then he spun, one hand on his hip, one diving into his hair.

She struggled in silence as he began pacing again. She heard him groan as he whirled then suddenly slammed his fists on kitchen counter. They made a terrible hollow sound, one that stabbed straight into her heart.

"I can have a DNA test back in as little as ten days," she said softly. His hands braced wide on the cold, marble surface, head dipped as her every nerve ending teetered on a thin tightrope, waiting for him to say something. She'd done the right thing. So why did it feel as if she'd ripped her world apart?

When the knock on her door came, they both jumped.

Melanie stood on the doorstep, holding Bella. "I thought I heard you come in and..." She trailed off as she spotted Alex.

Yelena ignored the question in her eyes, instead cupping Bella's warm head with a smile. "Could you give me some time, Mel? I'm in the middle of a situation here."

"You okay?" Yelena's nod only brought forth a frown. "Are you—"

"I'm fine," Yelena said softly. "Half an hour, okay?"

"Okay."

After her neighbor left, Yelena gently closed the door and turned back to Alex. He had his back to her, studying her photo array on the armoire.

Curious, she moved closer.

He held a silver frame with a picture of a smiling Bella in a pink romper suit.

She glanced up at him, expecting a scowl. But what she saw flipped her heart in her chest, making her breath stumble.

"I thought she'd killed him."

Confusion fuzzed her brain. It took a moment to realize he was talking about his parents.

"Alex." She reached for his hand, her fingers enveloping his. "Pam did it for you, to clear you once and for all. She found him floating in the pool at eleven-fifteen p.m. From the autopsy report, his time of death was eleven-twenty."

"So if she'd called an ambulance, he'd still be alive," Alex said softly.

"Maybe. It's hard to say."

"I thought…"

"That she'd pushed him into the pool?"

He nodded, staring at the picture of Bella before putting it back.

"And you were covering for her with your silence."

He didn't respond, just pulled his hand free and sat heavily on her sofa.

"Alex. Your mother's going in to make an official statement tomorrow and we have a top criminal lawyer on the case. But what she really needs is your support."

When he looked up, the bleak look in his eyes squeezed the breath from her chest.

"Of course."

The desperate urge to throw her arms around him, to soothe his pain until he was her old Alex, the laughing, teasing man who'd flirted with abandon and made love to her with wild passion, swamped every muscle in her body.

"Alex…" She paused, the words hovering on her tongue. But the longer the silence lengthened, the more fear took over. Instead, she said, "Do you want to do the DNA test? To make sure that Bella…" She flushed as he looked up. "Of course, I'll completely understand if you choose not to."

He quickly stood, an oddly graceful movement for such a big man. "Yelena. Do you honestly think I could live with myself not knowing?"

The raw honesty blazing from his bright eyes humbled her. "I thought maybe…"

"That I'd ignore my own child?"

The horrible truth slammed into her full force. She may be Bella's mother on paper but if Alex wanted to fight for custody, blood would win out every time.

"What?" Alex frowned as he watched Yelena's face drain of all color. "Yelena?"

She shoved her hair back, flicking it off her neck with an efficient sweep. With hands on hips, she looked him straight in the eye, the cool expression belying her compressed lips, the worry lines creasing her brow. "What?"

Clarity dawned, softening his expression. "I'm not going to take Bella from you."

Her eyes sparked. "No, you're not."

A small involuntary smile escaped him. He'd no doubt she would fight him with every breath in her body. That was his Yelena.

His heart soared then, forcing his body into a familiar thrum, even as his grin made her frown. It just amused him more.

"I love you."

From the frozen look on her face, he'd stunned her. Hell, he'd stunned *himself.* He hadn't meant to own up to it right here, right now, but somewhere in these last few minutes he realized he'd be a coward if he didn't.

Yet she whirled away, arms crossed, head bowed as if seeking divine guidance. The silence grew—an uncomfortable, expectant silence that gnawed at his control. He'd said it and all he'd gotten was a big fat nothing.

Finally, with her back still to him, she broke it.

"Don't, Alex. My brother is trying to destroy your family and—"

"This has nothing to do with Carlos."

She spun back around, her dark eyes riddled with skepticism.

It wounded him, knowing he'd put that look there. He said, "I called him this morning and offered him a deal. He could buy me out in exchange for me not charging him with slander."

"And?"

Alex raised one eyebrow. "He took it. With a few choice curses."

She said nothing, just considered his words in wary silence.

"Can we stop talking about your brother now?" he finally said. "This *really* isn't about him. I…" He paused, cleared his throat, straightened his shoulders and took his first ever leap of faith.

Gently capturing her wrists, he waited until she looked up. When their gazes met, his heart began to thump in earnest. Moment of truth.

"This is about you and me. You're fierce, loyal and passionate." He cupped her cheek, her soft, warm skin heating his palm. "My mother and Chelsea adore you. You were more than just a hired consultant—you were their friend."

"I still am," she choked out, blinking. To his surprise, Alex felt his eyes well in response. Dammit! Here he was in one of the most important moments of his life and he was about to stuff it up by *crying?*

He took a breath, wrestling for control. When he finally had it, he grasped both her arms and drew her closer. Tension tingled beneath his fingers, telling him her entire body was ready for flight. Her dark eyes held a stark vulnerability that touched him deep in his soul, called out to every primitive male instinct to protect her, keep her from pain and harm.

He'd willingly lay down his life for this woman.

"Yelena. I love being with you, love making love to you." He paused, alarmed to see a tear track slowly down her cheek. "I'd love to wake up with you every moment of my life. I love you." He brushed his thumb across her cheek, catching that tear in the silence.

With taut nerves and held breath, he waited. Finally, Yelena looked up through big, watery eyes, her mouth stretched into a wide, traffic-stopping smile. His heart stopped.

Yelena took a breath, a deep, jagged breath that felt like the first true one she'd taken in a long, long time. He looked so concerned, studying her with those bright blue eyes that held so much emotion, so much passion that she felt she'd explode with joy.

"Yes," she managed to say. "I love you, too."

When he cupped her face, her breath stuttered to a halt, her world shrinking to this one room, this one moment.

"I've loved you from the first moment I set eyes on you, Yelena Valero."

Love, hope and desire all surged up, threatening to choke her. But in the next instant his mouth came down on hers and joyous, life-giving breath filled her lungs.

Her lips parted beneath his, taking everything he offered with unabashed pleasure. It was more than she'd ever expected, had ever hoped.

Her desire ramped up as his mouth and tongue slowly explored hers, her breath and blood racing through her body, matching the joy in her heart.

"Please," came her breathy plea. "Please, Alex."

He cut her off with another kiss, just to feel her tremble beneath him. Then he cupped one generous breast, his fingers curling around the soft flesh, and deep male possessiveness surged up.

"Yelena, do you have any idea what you're doing to me?"

"Yes." Her satisfied smile sent his blood boiling, made his groin so hard he was amazed he didn't lose it right then.

He fumbled with her skirt, bunching it up around her waist as she went for his belt buckle. When the zipper slid down and her hand closed around him, the world seemed to stop spinning.

"Yelena," he managed to get out, his breath hoarse with

need. He needn't have said a thing—she stepped from her shoes, and pulled off her pantyhose in record time, then went down to the sofa, pulling him with her.

They kissed again, at first languorous, then more urgent, before Alex quickly stood and tugged off his pants, then pushed her down into the soft cushions.

Quickly he nudged her legs apart with his knee. She spread them willingly. He paused above her, weight straining on his arms as he stamped her passionate features in his brain. Bruised full lips, flushed high cheekbones, eyes black with desire. And that mass of curly dark hair, spread across the floor.

Then he thrust and she gasped, her eyes springing open before pleasure closed them again.

"Alex," she murmured, wrapping her arms around his neck, his name on her lips rocketing his need.

Together they moved, a slow, sensual motion that gradually surged and built until they were both slick with sweat, panting for release.

With her frantic breath in his ear, Alex gathered her up and rolled, and suddenly she was on top and he was deeper than he'd ever been.

She let out a gasp, her thighs tightening around his waist before quickly finding his rhythm. His hands grabbed her waist, rocking her back and forth. He was entranced by the look of utter pleasure on her face as she rode him.

A deep groan ripped him apart, pleasure afire in every muscle, every nerve. She kept the pace, her teeth biting down on her swollen bottom lip, her rapturous expression urging him on until he finally leapt over the edge.

Yelena collapsed on his chest, sweet satisfaction thrumming as their sweat and heat mingled. And as their breath heaved, the aftershocks hit, reverberating through her body, trembling every muscle.

Her cheek rested on his chest, his pounding heart in her

ear, the echoing beat still throbbing between her legs. When his arms tightened around her, blatantly possessive but still deeply satisfying, she took in a deep breath, their earthy scent of lovemaking filling her senses.

All hers.

They lay there as their heartbeats gradually returned to normal, until the sounds from the outside world began to filter in—the faraway hum and beep of traffic, the gentle whir from her fridge.

After a few moments Yelena reluctantly rolled onto her back with a satisfied sigh.

A deep laugh of realization rumbled in Alex's chest.

At her quizzical look, he grinned. "One day, my love," he said, placing a tender kiss on her forehead, "promise me we'll actually make it to a bed."

Yelena smiled back at him, her heart tight with happiness.

His mouth met hers in a laugh. "Deal."

Epilogue

Two weeks later Yelena propped her head up on her elbow, dragging the bed sheet up over her breasts with a satisfied sigh.

"That had to be the best lunch break ever."

In her bed Alex lay beside her on his back, sweaty and replete from their furious lovemaking. He laughed, a deep joyful sound that prompted her to join in. When their laughter finally faded, she placed a hand on his chest. The hot, tempered skin over corded muscle felt delicious. And it was all hers.

From their pile of clothes on the floor came a muffled ringtone.

"Yours," Yelena said, then after a confused pause, "and mine?"

"Sounds like it," Alex said, throwing off the sheet before getting to his feet. Yelena's mouth went dry. Her gaze brushed over his wide shoulders, down the smooth muscular back, tapering waist and beautifully curved buttocks before ending at the pair of extremely masculine legs.

A glorious sight indeed.

"You gonna get that?" Alex said, plucking the phone out of his jacket.

"Mmm-hmm."

"Yelena." The exasperation in his glance was tempered with mischief. "Your phone."

With a sigh, she pulled the sheet around her, left the warm bed and rummaged through her clothes on the floor.

"Hello?"

When she hung up, Alex was sat on the edge of her bed, a pair of cotton boxers spoiling her view. But the wide grin on his face compensated for all that.

"That was Mum. The Director of Public Prosecutions is willing to make a deal."

Her heart swelled as she padded over to him, tossing her phone on the bed. "Really? What's going to happen?"

His hands shot out, grabbing the front of her sheet. Slowly he pulled and she ended up wedged between his powerful thighs. "Her attorney's going to explain everything tomorrow but the bottom line is no jail time. The DPP is reluctant to try such a high-profile case that involves long-term spousal abuse."

The flinch barely reached his eyes but Yelena still saw it. She gently cupped his rough face in her hands. "That's wonderful. I'm so happy for her. And for you."

She leaned down. His lips were warm and pliant, meeting hers eagerly, and slowly they explored each other, soft flesh testing and tasting, breath merging as the kiss lengthened then deepened.

When his tongue tangled with hers, her blood went from languid lethargy to full boil. She'd never get enough of this, this glorious heat that only Alex seemed to arouse.

His arms encircled her waist, hands questing, and soon the sheet fell in a pool at her feet. Rough palms met her bottom and he gave an appreciative murmur.

"Alex?" she got out as his lips moved from her mouth to her neck.

"Mmm?"

"Don't you want to know about my call?"

Alex pulled her sharply up against him and was rewarded with her sudden gasp, one that eased into a groan as he leaned in and slid his mouth over one nipple.

He grinned against her silken skin. "Not really."

"It was—" he nipped at the hard pebbled nub and she gasped "—Jonathon."

He muttered something unintelligible, his mouth full of hot flesh. As the blood sped through every vein, stirring his manhood, he swept his palms over the twin globes of her butt.

Beautiful, just beautiful. And she was all his.

"I quit."

"Okay." He left her bottom, making his way up over her hips, the gentle indentation of her waist, her torso until—

She pulled back, his face firmly in her hands. "Specifically I quit your campaign."

He frowned, embers of desire burning the edges of his concentration. "What? Why?"

"Because a partner who sleeps with the clientele isn't the right image for Bennett & Harper."

"They didn't approve." His hands fell.

"No. So I quit."

He blinked, confused by her wide grin. "But you wanted that promotion."

Her expression softened. "But I want you more. And I actually like the idea of being my own boss."

His arms snaked back around her waist. "Say that again."

"I said, I'm going to start my own PR co—"

He pulled and she crashed into his chest, her hands

instinctively going out to temper the fall. But he quickly rolled and suddenly she was under him on the bed.

"And I want you."

Her mouth tweaked in impish delight. "So you'd better do something now you've got me."

Alex kissed her until they were both flustered and aroused, until his body screamed for release and his blood echoed loud and fast in his ears. He groaned when she took his earlobe between her teeth, gently nibbling.

Then Yelena said, "And one more thing. It arrived today."

She heard his breath snag. She didn't need to elaborate: reaching over to pull the large envelope from her night stand was explanation enough.

She repositioned the sheet around her body, took a cross-legged seat on the bed and offered the envelope. "Do you want to open it?"

He stared at her, his expression jumbled. Slowly he nodded, took the envelope, ripped it open and unfolded the contents in silence. Yelena fiddled with her necklace, chewing on her bottom lip as he read.

"Well?" she said after a moment. "What does it say?"

"Hang on."

She waited a few more impatient seconds. "Well?"

Shocked, Alex looked up, eyes wide as everything ground to a whirling halt. "Bella is mine."

Joy and amazement bubbled up in Alex's chest, widening his mouth, making his face ache with a broad grin. How many times had he wished he could rewind time, change the past? Yet for all those hollow wishes, everything from his roller-coaster life had brought him to this one amazing moment.

"So you're happy," she said slowly.

His joyous shout startled her, making him laugh. "Yelena, love, I am thrilled beyond words."

He grabbed her and planted a deep, warm kiss on her

mouth, his breath quickening when she responded without hesitation.

Then he pulled back, brushed the hair from her eyes. "I love you, Yelena."

"And I love you."

"You know what would make this moment perfect?"

Her dark eyes practically twinkled. "Food?"

"No." He chuckled. "I was thinking more along the lines of 'let's get married' but I guess I could go a burger or—"

"Are you serious?" Her eyes rounded in a way that made his groin tighten in excited expectancy.

He grinned. "Yeah, I'm actually pretty hungry."

"Alex!" She thumped him on the shoulder, way too soft to do any kind of damage. Then she continued, more soberly. "My brother was out to ruin you. My family staged an intervention, remember?"

He cupped her cheek in his palm, savoring the feel of her soft, warm flesh in his. "And I am stunned and humbled that you chose me."

"It wasn't difficult." And, Yelena realized as she gazed into his eyes, it was the truth. Since their ultimatum, the Valeros had at first tried to lay down the law, alternately threatening then cajoling. At her impassive silence, they'd grudgingly agreed to announce Gabriela's death if she'd reconsider her stance. Yelena had thanked them and offered to write the release but on everything else she refused to bend.

Alex was all she'd ever wanted.

"So isn't it about time you became part of my family?"

The pure, unadulterated love radiating from him choked the very breath from her lungs. Was it possible to have too much joy?

Slowly she leaned forward, kissed him gently on the lips.

"I love you, Alex. I'd marry you tomorrow if we could."

He grabbed her, his murmur of triumph warm against her mouth. "I'm sure we can work something out."

As desire swiftly rushed in, Yelena realized that throughout every trial she'd faced, every hardship, fantasies still came true. And then all thought fled as Alex proceeded to show her a few of his own.

* * * * *

COMING NEXT MONTH

Available July 13, 2010

#2023 THE MILLIONAIRE MEETS HIS MATCH
Kate Carlisle
Man of the Month

#2024 CLAIMING HER BILLION-DOLLAR BIRTHRIGHT
Maureen Child
Dynasties: The Jarrods

#2025 IN TOO DEEP
"Husband Material"—Brenda Jackson
"The Sheikh's Bargained Bride"—Olivia Gates
A Summer for Scandal

#2026 VIRGIN PRINCESS, TYCOON'S TEMPTATION
Michelle Celmer
Royal Seductions

#2027 SEDUCTION ON THE CEO'S TERMS
Charlene Sands
Napa Valley Vows

#2028 THE SECRETARY'S BOSSMAN BARGAIN
Red Garnier

HARLEQUIN®

A Romance

FOR EVERY MOOD™

Spotlight on

Heart & Home

Heartwarming romances
where love can happen
right when you least expect it.

See the next page to enjoy a sneak peek
from Silhouette Special Edition®,
a Heart and Home series.

*Introducing McFARLANE'S PERFECT BRIDE
by USA TODAY bestselling author Christine Rimmer,
from Silhouette Special Edition®.*

Entranced. Captivated. Enchanted.

Connor sat across the table from Tori Jones and couldn't help thinking that those words exactly described what effect the small-town schoolteacher had on him. He might as well stop trying to tell himself he wasn't interested. He was powerfully drawn to her.

Clearly, he should have dated more when he was younger.

There had been a couple of other women since Jennifer had walked out on him. But he had never been entranced. Or captivated. Or enchanted.

Until now.

He wanted her—*her,* Tori Jones, in particular. Not just someone suitably attractive and well-bred, as Jennifer had been. Not just someone sophisticated, sexually exciting and discreet, which pretty much described the two women he'd dated after his marriage crashed and burned.

It came to him that he…he *liked* this woman. And that was new to him. He liked her quick wit, her wisdom and her big heart. He liked the passion in her voice when she talked about things she believed in.

He liked *her.* And suddenly it mattered all out of proportion that she might like him, too.

Was he losing it? He couldn't help but wonder. Was he cracking under the strain—of the soured economy, the McFarlane House setbacks, his divorce, the scary changes in his son? Of the changes he'd decided he needed to make in his life and himself?

Strangely, right then, on his first date with Tori Jones, he didn't care if he just might be going over the edge. He was having a great time—having *fun*, of all things—and he didn't want it to end.

Is Connor finally able to admit his feelings to Tori, and are they reciprocated?
Find out in McFARLANE'S PERFECT BRIDE
by USA TODAY *bestselling author Christine Rimmer.*
Available July 2010,
only from Silhouette Special Edition®.

SSEEXP0710